T0270647

ALSO BY MICHELLE BENNINGTON

Devil's Kiss
Widow's Blush

THE HAZARDOUS HOARDING MYSTERIES

DUMPSTER DYING

MICHELLE BENNINGTON

KEYLIGHT
BOOKS
AN IMPRINT
OF TURNER
PUBLISHING

KEYLIGHT BOOKS
AN IMPRINT OF TURNER PUBLISHING COMPANY
Nashville, Tennessee
www.turnerpublishing.com

Dumpster Dying: A Hazardous Hoarding Mystery

Cover art by M. Wayne Miller
www.mwaynemiller.com
Book design by Ashlyn Inman

Library of Congress Control Number: 2024938585

9798887980225 Paperback
9798887980232 Hardcover
9798887980355 Epub

Printed in the United States of America

This book is dedicated to my mom.
I hope to become even half the woman you are.
(Proverbs 3:15)

1

enny Wiley eased her white Ford pickup truck into Uncle Mac's drive-thru behind an SUV. An emerging sunrise pooled pink and gold over the horizon.

She squinted at the brightly lit menu. "You know what you want yet? You best get ready. We're up next."

Ida Mae Puckett, her older sister, fluttered the newspaper, folded it into a manageable size, and shined her travel-sized flashlight on the list of yard and garage sale advertisements. "We may be in luck." She pointed to a spot on the newspaper. "Here's one on Birchfield Lane that doesn't say a thing about early birds." She circled the spot with a pen.

Henny and Ida Mae prided themselves on being the earliest of the early birds—the very bane of any yard sale host's existence—ready and waiting in driveways and hovering around garage doors near the break of dawn, long before sellers even set out their wares. The sisters had carried on this tradition of breakfast, yard sale shopping, and lunch every Saturday for a quarter of a century. And since they opted for an early retirement from their respective library and teaching positions at the Plumridge Elementary and High School, they didn't see any reason to put aside the tradition.

"Looks like a good one?"

Ida Mae paused and read some more. "I think so. It says, 'home and office furniture, adult and children's clothing, antiques, tools, dishes, knick-knacks, sporting goods, exercise equipment, and much more.'"

"Good. We'll hit that one first." Henny gazed at the menu. "I can't see a thing out of these glasses." She cleaned them on her pink seersucker blouse, then plopped them back on her nose. "I think I'm going to have that sausage biscuit combo with coffee. Uncle Mac's has good coffee. Do you know what you want?" She adjusted her pink Daytona Beach ball cap, tucking the sides of her unruly hair underneath.

Ida Mae looked up and leaned her large bosom over the console to study the menu. Her gray hair frizzed out of a white Commonwealth College Colonels visor, though the sun wouldn't be out for at least an hour. "I reckon I'll have the same." She sat up with a soft grunt.

The vehicle in front of them moved. Henny eased the car forward and lowered her electric window. The morning air hung fresh and warm for early October, nothing unusual for an Indian summer in Kentucky. The crickets sang out, competing with the soft-spoken man asking for her order. Henny shouted their choices at the speaker, paid, and collected the food.

They pulled into a parking spot at the side of the building, where, like a couple of conjurers, they mixed and stirred the exact amounts of sugar and cream into their cups to perfect the potent brew to carry them through hours of yard-saling.

Henny sipped her coffee through the hole in the plastic lid, appreciating the stillness of pre-dawn Plumridge—a small town wedged between the slightly larger bedroom community of Berryville and the city of Lexington in the lush bluegrass region of Kentucky.

Ida Mae gobbled her sausage biscuit, leaving a trail of crumbs down her ample bosom while she worked the cryptogram on the puzzle page. A wad of food in her doughy jaw, she muttered, "I don't know why I mess with these things. I'm not very good at them."

"Whichever letter appears most often is the 'E.'"

Ida Mae rolled her eyes. "Everybody knows that."

In a couple of bites, Henny scarfed her hash brown, then dove into the bag to retrieve her sausage biscuit. Her mind turned to her late husband, Walter, a whiz with crossword puzzles. Henny tried to work them, but soon gave up.

She stuffed the last bit of biscuit into her mouth, washed it down with some coffee, and started the car. "We need to get a move on."

Henny made a right onto Maple Street. They passed silent houses nestled under shade trees, some dark, some with porch lights on, some with only a kitchen window lit, signaling the gradual awakening of the town. She turned right again onto Main Street, which transformed into a roundabout encircling the Plumridge courthouse—a red-brick, Federalist-style structure with a white domed top, reminiscent of Monticello. The perimeter of the roundabout comprised old Victorian and Edwardian buildings transformed into law offices, cafes, and boutiques. After taking the first street off the roundabout, they passed a mechanic shop, a tiny used-car lot, and a strip mall consisting of several stores. The brilliant yellow glow of the sign above the Afford-A-Lot general store beckoned her. She slowed down. One of the best dumpsters in town, and Henny always found it optimal to visit on the weekend after their new shipments came in.

She glanced at Ida Mae, who glared at her. "Henrietta Marie Wiley. Don't you even think about it. You're not about to drag me on some fishing expedition in a dumpster."

Fine. The skin tightened between Henny's shoulder blades. Best to work without Ida Mae, anyway. She ruined all the fun with her fussing and her judgment. She gripped the steering wheel until her knuckles ached.

The first yard sale swept Henny's darkening mood away, like the sun bursting out of a cloud. Once she waded into all the figurines, books, records, and clothes, her mind emptied completely so that only a soft, numbing buzz remained. Henny's hands itched. Her eyes widened in anticipation, as if at a glorious Thanksgiving buffet. All she could eat, contain, stuff, hold, and carry.

Henny circled the tables over and over. She didn't know what she wanted but waited for a sign to come. And it did. A small wooden box. She opened it, revealing a petite angel with long, flowing blonde hair holding a red bird like a heart to the sky.

"It plays music," the yard sale host said from his lawn chair. "Bought that for our daughter a long time ago. She doesn't want it anymore, I reckon." The man's mud-caked boots crossed at the ankles, and his working-man's hands rested on his belly.

Henny wound it up and watched the angel twirl. "How pretty," she breathed. She knew exactly the person to give this to.

"Sell it to you for five bucks."

Henny waited for the angel to stop dancing. "I'll give you three."

"Deal."

IN A WHIRLWIND of bargain shopping and haggling, Henny and Ida Mae hit all the best yard sales in the best neighborhoods in Plumridge, and neighboring Berryville, before noon. For lunch, they treated themselves to the broccoli and cheese soup and steak sandwich deal at the Fig Tree Cafe in Berryville, and then ran by the Dollar Tree for gift wrap supplies before returning to Plumridge.

On the way home, Henny slapped the steering wheel. "Oh, shoot. I need gas."

She pulled into the Plumridge Pit Stop, a convenience store and liquor market known to locals as The Pit Stop, filled her tank, and pulled from her bag of newly acquired treasures the small jewelry box with the twirling angel inside.

Henny reached around to pull the Dollar Tree store bag from the backseat and wrapped it in white tissue paper.

"What are you doing?" Ida Mae asked.

"I'm going to give this to Jenna."

"Why?"

Heat rose in Henny's chest. Ida Mae's tone reeked of judgment. "Because I want to. Okay?"

"Fine by me." Ida Mae lifted her hands in surrender.

Henny stuffed the box down inside a metallic-red gift bag and hung it around her wrist while she filled up the tank. She spoke to Ida Mae through the opened window. "Wait here. I'll be right back.

You need anything?"

"No. Hurry up. I need to pee."

"You can pee inside."

Ida Mae screwed up her face. "I don't want to get out of the truck. And I definitely don't want to use that bathroom. It smells like deer urine."

Henny scurried inside. Even though she just ate lunch, she needed a half gallon of vanilla ice cream to go with the blackberry cobbler at home for their tradition of finishing off a day of shopping with dessert and coffee while they discussed their bargain hauls. Jenna Lawson stood behind the counter, ringing up another customer's purchase while they chatted about the weather and school and whatnot. Jenna smiled and waved as Henny passed the counter.

Henny clutched the handles of the gift bag as she searched the row of glass cooler doors for the ice cream. She grabbed a carton of vanilla and cradled it in her free arm.

Jenna beamed and stepped from behind the counter. She wore a thin cream and black sweater and faded black jeans that tapered above a pair of glittery red shoes. Beautiful, glittery red, like Dorothy's ruby slippers.

"I love your shoes!"

Jenna glanced at her feet. "These old things?" She flipped a tress of her long, perfectly coiffed platinum waves over her shoulder. "How are you? I haven't seen you in at least a week." She opened her arms wide to receive an awkward hug around the ice cream carton. Jenna stuck out like a swan among the ducklings at The Pit Stop, with her 1940s screen-siren flair and sweet nature.

Maternal feelings oozed through Henny's core. They separated, and Henny offered Jenna the gift bag. "I hope you like it."

Jenna gaped with surprise. "A gift?"

"It's not much."

Jenna pulled the tissue paper from the bag and removed a small rectangle jewelry box. She opened it to reveal the porcelain angel with flowing blonde hair. "Aw. I love angels. It's so pretty. Thank you."

"It reminded me of you because of your long, blonde hair, and you once told me your mother liked red birds."

"You're right. She loved angels too. This will remind me of my momma, and you, every day. I'll put it next to my bed."

"It plays music too." Henny flipped it upside down to wind up the key on the bottom.

The notes of "Wind Beneath My Wings" floated out as the angel spun around with her little red bird, encouraging it to fly.

"I don't recognize the song."

"It's from one of my favorite movies. You should look it up."

"I will when my shift is up. Or if I get bored here." She held up the box, watching the little angel spin. "My momma collected angels."

"She did?" Henny gaped. "I'm a collector too."

"Oh? What do you collect?"

"*Wizard of Oz*. And Barbies. And antique dolls. I don't know what all. I have several collections." Ida Mae's voice popped into her head. *You're not a collector. You're a hoarder!* Henny struggled to hold back a sneer against her sister.

"That's so cool." Jenna nodded, genuinely interested. "I still have Momma's collection. Daddy couldn't bear to get rid of it after she died, so he gave them to me." She ran her finger around the edge of the box. "I can't wait for Christmas. I'll put up all the angel ornaments with *loads* of lights." She glanced at Henny. "Momma always loved having a *ton* of lights on the Christmas tree, and Daddy liked to tease her about the tree catching fire." She smiled, a small dimple forming in one cheek. "And when I put the tree up this year, I'm going to put this on a table right beside it." Jenna hugged Henny again. "Thank you so much. Today's been tough, and then here you come to brighten it up like always. It's as if my momma sent you to look after me."

"You're welcome, sweetie." When she met Jenna three years ago, Henny laid silent claim to the girl who lost her mother at a young age. She felt as if destiny put them together. "You know, I had a daughter once." Henny toyed with the edge of the ice cream container lid. "Lydia. She died as a baby."

Jenna's face softened with pity. "Oh—"

A car horn honked outside.

"That's Ida Mae." Henny plunked the container of ice cream on the counter. "I better hurry, or she'll have my hide. I'll come back tomorrow after church for my Sunday afternoon special." Henny always looked forward to her Sunday afternoons with Lifetime movies, chocolate, Funyuns, and scratch-offs.

Jenna laughed. "I'll have everything reserved for you right up here." She patted the counter beside her open textbook.

"You'll be here?"

"You know I will. Seems I practically live in this place."

Henny collected her bag. The truck horn sounded again. "Maybe I'll win big this time. Then I'll ditch this town for good."

Jenna cupped the music box between her hands. "You and me both."

Henny exited, passing a yellow sports car with tinted windows parked by the dumpster at the side of the building. Cigarette smoke wafted out the driver's side window.

A fizzling sensation lit up beneath her skin. Women's intuition. Perhaps even a mother's intuition. She didn't know *why* it bothered her, but without thinking, she backtracked, opened the store door, and stuck her head inside.

Jenna looked up from her book.

"You working alone tonight, hon?"

"Yup. As always."

"Be sure you keep a phone close by. Be real careful. Okay?"

Jenna stood and peered out the big window. "What's wrong?"

"I don't know. Can't explain it, but there's a car over here. It's probably nothing, but it's giving me the creeps."

Concern flooded the girl's features, and she grew still. "What kind of car?"

"A yellow sports-type thing."

Jenna blanched and touched the angel charm on her necklace as she stared at the store phone, considering something.

A desire to protect this girl came over Henny. "Maybe I'll go over there and see what's happening. Hold on." She started toward the car.

Ida Mae leaned over, honked the horn, and shouted out her window. "What in the seventh shade of Hades are you doing?"

"Shh!" Henny cut her hand through the air. As she neared the yellow car, the driver revved its engine and sped away. Henny couldn't see the license plate through all the black smoke. She returned to the store. "Maybe you should call the sheriff."

"No. That's okay. I'm fine."

The creeping feeling didn't subside. She stepped up to the counter and wrote her phone number on the back of her receipt. "If you need anything at all, call me."

Jenna tucked the paper into her textbook. "Okay. But I'm sure everything'll be fine."

2

enny couldn't sleep. Walter lay across the piles of stuffed shopping bags cluttering the couch behind her. He'd shown up at random times over the past five years. In the beginning, his appearance surprised and grieved her, but now, it felt sometimes like he never died at all. He howled Elvis Presley's "Are You Lonesome Tonight," whistling to fill in the words he didn't know. When sleep didn't work, she turned up the television to watch *Bewitched* on the classic television channel. But his singing drowned out the show. He worked her last nerve, and, at last, her patience snapped.

She turned around in her recliner and hissed, "If you're going to hang out here, at least keep it quiet so I can sleep, or watch TV."

In his best Elvis imitation, he said, "Sorry darlin'. This here's a haunting." He laughed and winked.

The TV images danced between the show, snow, and color bars as the lamp flickered on and off. She glanced at the clock. One in the morning. Walter appeared in his ghostly prime between midnight and three a.m. She moaned and clapped her hands over her face.

"Two more hours of this nonsense? Heaven help me, I can't take this anymore." Henny struggled to the edge of her seat, jammed the recliner footstool down into place, and picked her way from the piles of stuff in the living room through to the kitchen. She jerked on her jacket, stuffed her socked feet into her black gardening boots covered with white daisies, and grabbed her purse and keys.

Walter appeared in front of her, causing her to jump back. "Where you going?"

"You're going to have to haunt an empty house." She stuck her hand through his middle and pulled the door open, stepped into the crisp night air, and slammed the door shut.

Walter stared out the window as the porch light flickered like a strobe light.

"Put that in your pipe and smoke it," Henny muttered, trudging through the dew-laced grass toward her truck.

Agitated, sleepy, and angry, Henny knew only one thing to do. She cranked up the AC and drove to the closest shopping center.

Typically, Ladybug's Consignment held the title of her favorite place to dumpster dive, but since their delivery trucks came Monday, she felt it pointless trying to dive there before Tuesday. The best place for an early Sunday-morning dive tended to be the Hobby Hut in the shopping center on the outskirts of Frankfort, only about fifteen minutes from Plumridge. Their stock came on Fridays, making it the best weekend retreat for diving.

Henny pulled up behind the Hobby Hut, walked around to the back of the truck, and lowered the tailgate to extract her dive kit. She grabbed a sparkly pink messenger bag. She removed a headlamp from inside, turned it on, pulled it down over her unruly hair, then slipped on a pair of teal rubber gardening gloves. She hung the bag diagonally over her body and withdrew a white metal stepladder tied to a blue milk crate with a yellow boat line.

Henny approached her target, opened the stepladder, climbed up, and pushed open the dumpster's side door with some effort. She tossed the milk crate into the dumpster. She scanned the interior for dangerous objects and startled critters and then she drew her legs over the lip of the opening. Holding on to the edge, she dropped into the depths of plastic bags, Styrofoam, and packing peanuts. She pushed the items around. Nuts. Only a few tiny boxes and a smattering of discarded items. Henny spotted a ball of frayed yarn. Not too bad. She might be able to use that for something. She dropped the yarn inside her messenger bag and resumed her search. A few packets of flatback, multi-colored rhinestones looked good. A thin, open box revealed a broken frame. Just needed a bit of glue and some new rhinestones. She added the frame to her bag and continued sifting through the discarded treasures.

Her hands landed on another box, larger and filled with a cardboard divider. She opened the flaps. What a delightful find! She reached inside and pulled out a small porcelain angel ornament that fit neatly in her palm. She wore the prettiest red, sparkling dress. The dress reminded Henny of Jenna's glittery shoes.

The dive a success, Henny shifted bags to create a level spot and pulled on the yellow boat line to drag the stepladder inside with her. She dropped the milk crate to the ground outside and used the boat line to place it under the opening. She climbed onto her stepladder and, feeling around with her tiptoes, lowered herself onto the crate. She extracted her ladder and loaded up her kit. A perfect dumpster dive.

Only two a.m. She didn't want to deal with Walter, so Henny went to the Pancake Palace, ordered a decaf coffee and a pecan waffle, and ruminated on the joy of gifting Jenna with the angel.

AFTER CHURCH THE next day, Henny beelined to her truck so she could get to The Pit Stop. She needed to hurry because the darkening gray clouds threatened to release a heavy rain.

Ida Mae, a little out of breath, caught up to her in the parking lot. "What're you in such a rush for?"

"I need to get to The Pit Stop. Jenna's saving me a bag."

Her sister snorted. "A bag of what? You afraid they're going to run out of Funyuns?"

"None of your beeswax."

"Here we are, fresh out of church, and this is how you're acting."

"Then stop annoying me."

Ida Mae released a deep, throaty laugh. "You're battier than Mammoth Cave." She held the truck door so Henny couldn't shut it.

"I want to know why you're in such a hurry."

"I have a gift for Jenna. That's all. Is that okay with you, Nosie Rosie?"

"Jenna?" Ida Mae frowned, searching her memory. "That cashier girl?"

"Yes."

"Didn't you give her a gift yesterday?"

"So?"

Ida Mae lowered her voice. "Honey, this ain't right. Why you so fixated on that girl?"

"I'm not *fixated*. She's nice. We're friends. And she doesn't have a momma anymore . . . " She shrugged and dug her car key into her palm. "So . . . "

Pity pulled down the corners of Ida Mae's mouth. "Sweetie, she's not your child." She placed a plump hand on Henny's shoulder. "She's not Lydia."

White-hot rage flashed through Henny like a lightning bolt. "Don't you think I know that?" She brushed her sister's hand away. "Now stop touching me, and mind your business."

Shock knocked Ida Mae back a couple of steps as Henny reached for the door and slammed it.

Fueled now by anger instead of excitement, Henny raced through the streets toward the convenience store sitting on the edge of Plumridge, along the busy highway leading to Lexington. The rain began falling as she whipped the truck into the parking lot and sat there a moment, listening to the steady rhythm of the windshield wipers, and trying to shove the image of Ida Mae's judging eyes out of her mind. She looked down at the ornament in her palm.

"Jenna will appreciate this. I don't care what Ida Mae says." Henny released the last shaky breath of her anger and approached the convenience store.

The bell above the door clanged as a customer ducked his head to dash into the rain. Henny caught the door and swept inside.

"Hey there, Henny." Rhona Clark, a petite middle-aged woman with a gravelly smoker's voice, stepped briskly toward the counter from the direction of the back room. She carried a roll of register tape.

Blue sparks caught Henny's eye. Rhona wore glittery blue shoes identical to Jenna's red ones. How exciting! She watched the blue glitter flash and wink until they disappeared from sight behind the counter.

"I sure like your shoes. They're so pretty," Henny said.

"Thank you. Aren't they the sweetest? I found them out at the Bargain Barn. Only ten dollars. You want scratch-offs today?"

Henny shifted from side to side. "Sure do. My usual ones, and a lottery ticket."

"You got it. Let me get this tape changed." Rhona lifted the lid on the register and set about replacing the empty spool. "Hope you're not going yard-saling today in all this rain."

"I'm not that dedicated. Besides, Saturdays are the best days. I found all kinds of treasures yesterday."

"Did you, now? Well, that's good. I sure wish I could go yard-saling. My grandbaby could use some new onesies."

"I'll keep a lookout for you. If I see something, I'll pick it up, and you can pay me back."

"Bless your heart, I sure appreciate that. He's six months, and about fourteen pounds. And as round as a Butterball turkey." She cackled.

Henny tightened the hold on the angel figurine, the wing digging into her palm. "I hoped to see Jenna today."

"Oh, honey. I ain't seen her for a couple of weeks."

"Wh-what? Isn't she working today?" Henny ran the bumpy texture of the angel's wings between her finger and thumb.

"No, my manager called me at home and asked if I could come in because Jenna didn't show for her shift. That's why I didn't make church this morning." Rhona closed the lid on the register and began ringing up the purchase.

Henny muttered, "Mercy me..." Jenna certainly didn't seem like the sort of girl to take off without warning. "That doesn't seem like her."

"I know." Rhona pulled scratch-off tickets from the roll and rang them up.

Henny recalled the yellow car sitting outside the store last night. The one that gave her the creeps. "Do you know anyone who drives a yellow sports car?"

"What kind of sports car? Like a Corvette?"

Crap. Henny suddenly wished she paid more attention to her brother, Cash, when he jabbered on and on about cars. "Um...I saw one out here last night. With black stripes over the top, a flat front, and tinted windows."

Rhona murmured the details to herself. "Is that a Mustang? Or a Charger?"

"I don't know."

"I don't know anyone who drives something like that, though."

"I know she's taking classes at the community college. Maybe she studied for a test all night and fell asleep?"

"I doubt that. I think she dropped out of school."

"What? Are you sure?"

"I don't know, hon. She mentioned once she failed a couple class-es. Lately, she stopped bringing her books in."

"Maybe she managed a way to make up the classes? Last night I saw a textbook on this counter..." Henny poked the countertop.

"I believe you, hon. All I know is, a couple of months ago, she stopped talking about school right around the time she asked to take on more hours here. But Mark's as tight as a frog's bottom and re-fused to give her no more than thirty-five hours." Rhona shrugged. "Maybe she got another job. Can't say I blame her. Her daddy's sick so I know she needs the money."

Henny's shoulders tightened. A hectic feeling fluttered under her skin like a million butterflies.

The countertop around Rhona brimmed with scores of impulse purchases from lighters to candy, to magnets, to hemp bracelets. Henny's hands itched. She didn't like this feeling and ached to soothe it. Her eyes fell on a hemp bracelet with shiny purple beads down the center.

Henny picked up the bracelet, and the butterflies settled. She set it on the counter. "I need this too."

Rhona rang it up. "Anything else?"

The rain now pounded the windows.

Henny slipped the bracelet into her pocket and rolled the beads between her thumb and forefinger. "My Sunday special, please. Jenna set them aside for me."

Rhona searched under the counter and pulled out a bag of Funyuns, a king-sized Milky Way Midnight bar, and a Sunday newspaper chock-full of coupons and savings. "Is this it?"

"That's it." An image of Jenna smiling flashed through Henny's mind.

"That'll be twenty-seven ninety, hon."

Henny paid and started to leave but paused at the door. "If you see a bright yellow sports car lingering around here, get the license plate and let me know, will you? You have my number."

"Sure thing, hon."

Henny left the store, running through the rain. Through the chaos emerged a vague thought.

I warned her about that car. She didn't listen. Why didn't you listen to me, Jenna?

Henny's mind raced, and only one thing could calm it now. She drove quickly to her destination and parked. A banner flapped on the front of the Bargain Barn building, announcing a sale.

Henny slid out of her truck and ran through the rain as fast as her aching knees allowed, her pantyhose getting soaked in her shoes, and rain spattering her glasses. She searched her mind for an excuse, a reasonable reason, for Jenna's absence from work. Maybe an emergency with her daddy? Rhona said he suffered from poor health. She made it to the sidewalk under the portico and paused to wipe her glasses with the inside of her gray cardigan. Henny walked into the building and headed toward the shoe department, scanning all the boots, sandals, flats, platform shoes, and strappy heels, but she couldn't find any of the sparkling red shoes, those beautiful shoes like the ruby slippers Dorothy wore to skip along Oz's yellow brick road.

A sales lady, in a company polo and black pants, approached.

"May I help you?" she offered through a saccharine smile, her frothy frizz of blonde hair bouncing.

"A friend of mine bought red, sparkly flats here."

"Oh, yes. People love those shoes." She led Henny to a round, multi-tiered stand in the middle of an aisle. The stand sparkled like a Christmas tree in gold, silver, white, black, blue, copper, and pink.

"But there's no red. I really wanted red." Henny pouted.

The woman plastered on a tight smile. "That's our most popular color. We're sold out right now."

"Will you be getting more?"

"Our truck comes on Saturday."

"Okay, thank you. I'll be back." Henny turned to leave, but couldn't exit the store without a bag, so she bought a pair of silver angel earrings for Jenna for the next time she saw her.

Henny arrived home and tucked the earrings safely away, alongside the ornament. The rain drove against the house relentlessly, and thunder rumbled in the distance. Wind whipped through the trees, blowing colorful leaves to the ground. The petals of the plastic daisy pinwheel whirred, and the Terminix pest control sign in her front yard trembled. She watched the rain from the kitchen window while the coffee brewed and her apple crisp heated in the microwave. A chill rippled over her.

Walter popped up at her side. "Boo!" He cackled when she jumped. He snapped his fingers, bringing the coffee maker and the microwave to a halt. The kitchen drawers slid open when he wiggled his fingers. Silverware spilled out of a drawer and danced around the room.

Henny turned a worried gaze on him. "Can you please haunt me some other time?"

The silverware dropped back into the drawer, and the coffee maker and microwave powered up again. "What's the matter, sweetie?"

"Jenna Lawson didn't show up to work today."

He shrugged. "Who's that?" He edged his pipe out of the front pocket of his bib overalls.

An edge entered her voice. "I told you about her. The cashier out at The Pit Stop."

"Oh. The one you think is our daughter." He lit the pipe, the scent of cherry pipe tobacco competing with the coffee and apple crisp.

Normally, she enjoyed the scent and didn't mind him smoking inside, but he'd touched a nerve. She slapped the countertop. "Must you smoke that blasted pipe all the time? And can't you go outside with it? And how come I'm the only one who smells it? Ida Mae never says a word."

"I don't know the ghost smell laws. Maybe because she's not a believer. But yelling at me won't change the fact that that Jenna girl doesn't belong to you."

Henny's voice raised to a squeaky pitch. "I never said she did. And I don't know why you're attacking me and being so ugly. She'd be the same age as Lydia. They might be friends."

"Honey . . . " The playfulness dropped from Walter's voice, and it took on a somber quality. "You need to let go of all that. Get some distance from her. She's a twenty-three-year-old stranger. She's not your daughter, and she can't possibly be your friend. Not really. There's too much age difference."

"Leave me alone. Just leave me alone!" Henny pushed her way past the boxes and bags in the kitchen and hallway and locked herself in the bathroom.

When she came out, miraculously, Walter didn't make a peep the rest of the night.

3

What a bleak week of rain and worry. Henny wanted to visit The Pit Stop, but Walter's words struck a nerve, so she settled for calling to check on Jenna. No luck. Henny paced, watched TV, ate, and organized her recent acquisitions of baby clothes and toys by stacking the bags neatly in the corner of the master bedroom where the bassinet sat buried for the past several years.

By Friday evening, she felt more like herself and eager for Saturday. Yard Sale Day. Her favorite day. *Family Feud* blared in the background while she nibbled at a grilled cheese sandwich and some BBQ Fritos. Henny crunched her chips and scrolled through the images on her phone. One of Jenna from Halloween last year when she dressed in a long, pink gown as Barbie, her hair in voluminous blonde curls. Another where Jenna dressed in U of B basketball garb to celebrate their placement in the NCAA Final Four Championship games. And still another when she playfully donned a floppy straw hat Henny scored at a yard sale.

Loneliness and worry yawned inside Henny. *Jenna, where are you?*

"I'll find you," Henny murmured, studying the picture. "Flyers!" she said suddenly, launching herself out of the recliner, and nearly dumping her food on the floor. "I'll make flyers. I'll print off these pictures and pin them up all around town. I'm going to be out tomorrow, anyway. Ida Mae will help."

Walter popped in. "What're you up to?"

"I want to help find Jenna by putting flyers up all over town tomorrow."

"That's a good idea. What does her family say about it?"

"Surely, they won't mind the help."

"Unless someone in her family did something to the girl."

Oh. Yeah. Henny watched enough *Dateline*, and read enough true crime books, to know people closest to a missing person are often responsible. "You're right. I'll get her daddy's phone number and talk to him first."

Walter stretched out on the couch, puffing his pipe and filling the air with the sweet aroma. He wiggled his fingers and flipped the television channel to *Gunsmoke* on TMC.

Henny grabbed a notebook from the junk drawer in the kitchen. "You're going to look for her on your side, aren't you?" she asked, as she dialed The Pit Stop.

"Of course. Though I hope she doesn't end up here any time soon."

Henny felt the cold, heavy weight of that statement. "Me too."

Someone answered the phone.

"Who am I speaking with? Hey, Rhona. This is Henny Wiley. Can I get the phone number for Jenna Lawson's daddy's place?"

When she hung up with Rhona, she dialed Mr. Lawson and explained how she wanted to help.

His voice quivered. "Oh, bless you, Mrs. Wiley. You might be an angel. I can't get around like I used to."

"Don't you worry about it one bit. I'll take care of everything. I only need some information from you." Henny collected all the pertinent information that goes on a Missing Persons flyer.

"Have you reported her missing yet?" she asked.

"I have. But to be honest, they don't seem too concerned. They said she's probably run away or gone off with a guy. Or maybe some friends. The sheriff says he's putting a deputy on it, but no one's contacted me yet."

"Well, I'm sure everything will be okay, Mr. Lawson. Don't you worry."

BLESSED SATURDAY ROLLED in on sunbeams and with a light fog. Henny rose as the first pink light of dawn blushed on the horizon, too excited to sleep, and eager to get started on hanging flyers. Ida Mae walked in with a bag of chicken biscuits, potatoes, and coffee from Jolene's Chicken Shack, commonly known as Jolene's. Standing near the kitchen table, piled with books, bags, dishes, and empty containers, they wolfed down their breakfast.

As they left the house, Ida Mae said, "First we need to hit Thornberry Court. They say they have drapes. I need new ones."

They stepped through the damp grass toward Henny's truck. Mist rolled across the fields behind her house. The land once belonging to Walter's family. She noticed a bulldozer in the distance, and an aching yawn opened up inside her. Right now, she enjoyed the spacious yards in her neighborhood and could live without a bunch of nosy neighbors watching everything she did. But soon they planned on tearing down the barn that no longer belonged to her. The barn that recorded the years of Walter's life and work. She hoped Walter could forgive her. Someday.

A chill hung in the air, so they both wore jeans, T-shirts beneath cardigans, and ball caps. Kentucky Octobers could be unpredictable. A crisp morning might quickly ascend into the seventies, so dressing in layers made sense.

Henny clutched the flyers to her chest. "Ida Mae, something just awful happened. Jenna, my cashier friend from The Pit Stop, is missing. I spoke with her daddy, and he gave me permission to put up some flyers for her."

"Oh, Henny, that's terrible. I'll help any way I can. Can we hang them as we go?"

"Of course. But I want to stop at a couple places on the way to Thornberry Court."

"Henny, there are four good yard sales. If we don't get there early, we're going to miss out on the best stuff. You know how it is this time of year."

"I know. But this is more important. Besides, the October sales are always a little iffy." Yard sale season usually wrapped up by the end of October, but if the weather held, Henny and Ida Mae might get a couple more Saturdays to hunt for treasure. Regardless, the October yard sales usually offered the least amount of desirable items, as the sellers made their last-ditch efforts to unload their junk before winter set in.

On the way to the Thornberry Court sale, they stopped by The Pit Stop, passed flyers out to people getting gas, and hung them up in the store windows and on the doors, so Jenna's smiling face greeted each visitor.

Afterward, the sisters proceeded with their treasure hunt. They waded through three meaty yard sales, one wimpy one, and a small flea market in Berryville, spending the entire afternoon picking through knick-knacks, clothes, dishes, and other whatnots.

Now tired and peckish for a mid-afternoon sweet treat, they headed toward Henny's house, but as they passed the Bargain Barn, Henny remembered the shoes.

She slowed down and pulled into the parking lot. "I need to go in here for a minute."

"What for?"

"There's a pair of shoes I want."

Henny and Ida Mae entered the store, now decked out with displays of Halloween and autumn-themed clothes, home decor, and an aisle dedicated to costumes for children, adults, and pets. On a mission, Henny marched to the sparkly shoe display, circling it around and around. Unable to find the red shoes, she spoke to a clerk, only to discover the day's delivery did not include them.

Fire sprang up in Henny's chest and spread over her upper body to the roots of her hair. "One of your employees told me to expect them today."

The clerk shrugged her shoulders. "We have no way of knowing what's coming in."

"So, there's no red sparkly shoes?"

"Not on this truck. Maybe next week."

"Fine." Henny strode to the front door.

Ida Mae tripped along after her.

"Sometimes, it takes a little longer. I'm sure they'll eventually get them."

"Maybe they will, and maybe they won't." Henny, near tears by the time they reached the truck, slammed the door and peeled out of the parking lot.

"Well, I don't know what the big deal is." Ida Mae clipped her seat belt into place and grabbed the roof handle. "It's a pair of shoes."

Henny shot rapid-fire blinks at her sister. "I need a pair of those sparkly shoes. The next time I visit The Pit Stop, Jenna and I can laugh about being red-glitter shoe twins!"

Ida Mae held up her hands in surrender. "Okay, okay. It's going to be okay."

"Hmph. We'll see."

They flew through town, where Halloween and autumn decorations appeared in the form of vinyl window clings, orange and black ribbons tied around lamp posts, and planters full of mums. As Henny popped around a curve, she noticed the dated shopping plaza containing her favorite dumpsters. Only one thing could calm her now. She swung into the parking lot.

Ida Mae applied her imaginary brakes and clutched the door handle. "What the Sam Hill are you doing?"

Henny looked down her nose, over the dash. "We need to post flyers here. This is a busy place." Henny, itching for a dumpster dive, knew she needed to finish her duty to Jenna first. They floated past the White Lotus Spa, where the pink neon Open sign flickered in the curtained window, by Sassy Styles hair salon, commonly known as Sassy's, and past Ladybug's Consignment shop.

Henny parked the truck. Picking up the flyers, she divided them. "You take these and put them on windshields. I'll take the rest into the stores."

They separated to finish distributing the papers. Every store Henny entered heartily agreed to post the handout in their windows and on their doors. Only one location left—the White Lotus Spa.

Henny approached the White Lotus and entered the building. A young woman stood behind the counter—short and petite, with long black hair as fine and shiny as corn silk.

The girl smiled at her. "May I help you?"

Henny put the flyer on the counter. "This girl is missing. Her name is Jenna Lawson. Have you seen her?"

The girl's eyes darted. "I'm sorry. I don't know her."

"Please look again. Are you sure?"

The girl glanced at the sheet and smiled once more. "I'm sorry. I don't know anything about it. Do you have an appointment?"

"No. I don't have an appointment, and I don't want one. I want to know what happened to this girl." She poked the paper. "Right here."

A stout woman with a doughy chin, frosted blue eyes, and an icy stare exited the back room. "What's going on?" Her snarl curled into a forced smile.

Henny lifted the flyer up. "This is Jenna Lawson. Have you seen her?"

The younger girl shifted to the side and made herself busy as the older woman took her place. "No, not in a while." She spoke in sweet tones, but the sweetness didn't match the coldness of her stony eyes.

Henny flinched. So the younger girl had lied. "What do you mean, in a while? I just asked her"—she pointed at the younger girl—"and she said she doesn't know her. Which is it?"

"She's a client."

Henny gasped. "What?"

The phone rang, and the younger girl rushed to answer it.

The older woman braced herself against the counter. "Ma'am, if you aren't purchasing a service, I must ask you to leave."

"Please, just tell me—"

"Ma'am, please leave."

Talk about a brick wall. Henny struggled to think straight. "Fine. I'll leave. Will you at least hang this notice in your window?"

"Sure," the lady cooed, "we'd love to help in any way we can."

As Henny exited the store, she glanced back through the window to see the woman wad up the flyer and throw it away.

Henny's heart sank in exact measure to the anger rocketing up-ward and exploding in her brain. "How dare she—" She spun around to go back in when Ida Mae called out to her.

"Hey, Henny. I passed out all my papers. You have any more?"

Henny fumed at the White Lotus storefront, rolling the flyers in her fist. She joined Ida Mae to help her.

With the job done, they climbed back into the truck. Henny glared at the White Lotus. Dark, prickly agitation spiked her blood and scraped through her veins. For a moment, she imagined driving her truck right through the front window and over that brick wall of a woman who threw away Jenna's flyer. Henny closed and opened her fingers over the steering wheel.

"What's wrong with you?" Ida Mae asked, flapping the neck of her shirt to fan herself. "Why're you so quiet?"

Henny needed release, a curative to push the bad thoughts from her mind. "I have one more thing to do." She started the truck and maneuvered it around the side of the building toward the back.

"Oh," Ida Mae said flatly, as realization settled on her. "Sweet brown sugar, Henny. Dumpster diving?"

"Only for a minute. I want to take a peek."

"When are you going to quit this? We went to several yard sales and a huge flea market today. You don't need to do this."

"All I need is a peek, Ida."

They edged around the back of the building where a dumpster stood, cast in golden light behind the consignment shop.

"I can't *be-lieve* you're doing this. In broad daylight?" Ida Mae sunk down in her seat. "This is so embarrassing. I could just die..."

"Hush," Henny snipped as she jammed the gearshift into park. "We're behind the building, so I don't know who you think is going to see you, duchess." She left the truck running.

"It'll only take a minute." Henny opened the door and slid out of the truck.

"Fine. I'll be lookout." Ida Mae followed reluctantly, looking around, as if expecting to be ambushed.

Henny scurried like a mouse around to the back of the truck to grab her diving kit. The sparkly pink messenger bag slung over her body, and gardening gloves on, she carried it to the dumpster. She set up her stepladder, slid open the door, and dropped her milk crate inside. Seeing nothing worth diving for yet, she grabbed a broken broom handle and used it to shift a few boxes. Some empty beer cans and a Happy Pappy bourbon bottle. Fast-food bags, cigarette butts, garbage—the typical stuff. Nothing she wanted. About to turn away from the bin, a red spark caught her eye.

Henny turned back. Standing on her tiptoes on the top step of the ladder, she leaned further inside the dumpster. Something glittery. She leaned further in, reaching with her broken broom handle, but couldn't make contact. "Dang it. All right then." She grabbed the top of the dumpster, lifted herself to sit in the opening, and lowered herself inside.

Ida Mae covered her face. "Oh my stars. I hope no one we know comes rolling through."

Henny landed on a crumpled cardboard box. She shifted the bags and discarded food containers to the side to reveal the object. A shoe.

A red, glittery ballet flat, exactly like the ones Jenna wore, and the very style Henny searched for at the Bargain Barn. On closer inspection, Henny noticed the brand name looked rubbed off. She flipped the shoe over, seeing a scruffy worn-thin bottom.

Someone loved this shoe, wearing it nearly to scraps. She tucked it into her messenger bag and searched for the other one. Henny needed that shoe. She threw boxes and papers and bags aside, digging down deep until her nails scraped the metal bottom of the dumpster.

Ida Mae's voice echoed in the metal chamber. "Get out of there. If someone sees you, they'll think you're crazy as a bed bug."

Henny's head throbbed with the exertion. "Fine. I can't find the dadgummed thing, anyway."

"What?"

"The other shoe." She switched out her crate and stepladder and lifted herself into the opening as Ida Mae stepped back.

"Don't you think you're too old to be doing this? Someday, you're going to fall and break a hip in one of those things, and the garbage men will find you—that is, if they don't crush you in their truck first."

Henny straightened her glasses. "Oh, you're so dramatic." She stepped onto solid ground, gathered up her kit, and marched toward the truck.

Ida Mae followed. "Are you seriously keeping an old shoe you dug out of the garbage?"

"Yes. I am." Henny tossed her diving kit into the bed, along with the broom handle, thinking it might be useful later, and climbed into the truck.

Ida Mae clambered into the passenger side with a grunt, slamming the door behind her. "That's disgusting. There's no telling where that came from. What on earth do you want with *one* old shoe from a garbage dump?"

"I want it because it's pretty. Everyone needs pretty things occasionally. And I deserve pretty things as much as anyone else. I'm just sorry I didn't find its mate."

"Hmph." Ida Mae crossed her arms over her chest. "You're liable to find more than that someday. No good can come of poking around dumpsters."

4

After a stop at Jolene's to get takeout for supper, Henny and Ida Mae returned to Henny's house. The town pre-dated the Civil War by almost a century and saw little change in the decades following. The town council and citizens wanted it that way, preferring to let cities like Lexington and Louisville have all the growth and development they could handle, while Plumridge wanted to maintain the charm of the small-town golden years gone by.

Henny's neighborhood dotted a decreasingly rural landscape. She remembered a time when her closest neighbor lived a mile away, but now, the houses sprung up like little mushrooms, almost overnight. Only a few farms in the area remained. Several of the homes displayed pumpkins and jack-o'-lanterns on their porches, and autumn or Halloween wreaths on their doors. A few went all out, creating entire Halloween scenes in their front yards with life-sized mummies rising out of caskets, vampires lurking behind tombstones, and witches dancing around cauldrons. On Halloween night, those yards became spectacles lit with purple or green lights, machines pumping out a blanket of fog, and recordings of creaky floors, wicked laughter, and ghostly shrieks playing over a loudspeaker. The children in the neighborhood flocked to those every year, and every year the Halloween revelry seemed to grow larger and spookier.

Henny's house, a white wood bungalow with black shutters, sported a green tin roof and a central dormer over the covered porch.

Hydrangea bushes edged the house, and a host of ceramic and plastic woodland creatures populated the yard around her Terminix sign. Henny made a mental note to pay her pest control bill. She liked to collect things, but bugs and rodents didn't need to be part of her collection. A pinwheel daisy stood by the driveway.

They eased up the gravel drive. Henny parked in front of the detached garage beside Ida Mae's maroon Buick LeSabre.

Ida Mae still fussed. "I don't know why you need that dirty old shoe. It's used, from a dumpster, not your size, and there's only one!" She opened the door and slid to the ground. Ida Mae reached in the back of the truck and pulled out the bags of things they purchased at the yard sale. She opened the back door to her own car. "I know you said you like pretty things, and I understand that, but it doesn't make any sense. What are you going to do with one old, dirty, used shoe?" She tossed her bags in the backseat and closed the door.

Henny carried the Jolene's bag loaded with the closest-to-homemade fried chicken, coleslaw, mashed potatoes, biscuits, and macaroni and cheese available.

Khan, a German shepherd mix, stood up on the porch of the gray house next door and barked his brains out, his tail waving wildly. He never left the porch but barked to wake the devil every time someone entered his field of vision.

Henny opened the back door. Ida Mae dumped Henny's purchases on the kitchen table, while Henny pushed back papers and dishes to clear a spot at the table.

Ida Mae muttered, "I swear, every time I come in here, there's twice as much stuff as the last time. Where're you getting all this? Why don't you get rid of some of it?"

Henny tried to tune out Ida Mae. She knew her collections bordered on out of control. After all, Walter reminded her at least once a week. In her lucid moments, an overwhelming urge to clean and organize poured over her. But such confusion mounted about where to even begin the behemoth task, that the desire became buried under a tidal wave of guilt, shame, and exhaustion. How could she throw away or sell an item or items she cherished? Besides, she might need something in the future for one of the scores of projects she planned on completing.

At any rate, what she didn't need is an older sister getting all high and mighty and acting like their mom. Ida Mae's nagging pressed like a finger on a festering wound, such that Henny could almost feel the pain, as the tension knotted between her shoulder blades and caused her hands to open and clench, open and clench.

"I don't want to hear it."

Ida Mae turned her head slowly to stare at her as if to say, *Just who do you think you are, Missy?*

Oops. Hush up, Henny. No point in getting into this now. "Let's eat some supper, and then we can have cobbler and coffee after. That'll be nice, won't it?" Henny pushed aside several cans of food, empty dishes, and knick-knacks to make a pot of coffee. "You want to make our plates? I want the leg or a thigh. Don't waste my time with the wings."

"How can you stand living with piles of stuff everywhere?" Ida Mae opened the bag and removed the bucket and sides, shoving things back to make room. "Maybe you should have a yard sale? You might make a ton of money."

"I don't want to have a yard sale," Henny said, standing on her tiptoes to search the cabinets. She turned to the pantry and dug the paper plates and coffee cups from their plastic sleeves. Thankfully, they had bought enormous cups of iced tea for their meal.

"I'll help you. I bet there's stuff you don't even remember buying."

"Don't worry about it. I'll get around to it." Henny scooped grounds into the coffee maker, filled the reservoir with water, and started the brew. She looked out the window above the kitchen sink, shame twisting in her gut. Henny dipped her hand in her pocket and touched the beads on her new hemp bracelet. Her stomach relaxed a little, but the pressure surged in her head.

To be truthful, Henny wanted to shove Ida Mae out the door and lock it behind her, but her momma's voice reminded her they ought to be kind to each other.

"I don't understand what you do with your money, hon. I mean, I know we go yard-saling every weekend, but I don't recall you buying *so much*. This is all coming from dumpsters, isn't it?" Ida Mae left the kitchen, headed for the sunroom. "I wonder just how much stuff you *do* have."

Before Henny could head her off at the pass, Ida Mae pushed open the door and gasped. She gazed upon the stacks of boxes and bags, toys, clothes, and pictures piled on the back porch. She shook her head. "Oh my goodness, Walter is rolling over in his grave."

Henny maneuvered around Ida Mae and grabbed the doorknob. "You hush up. You don't talk about that." She glared at her sister, boring holes into her.

"And Momma and Daddy are rollin' in their graves too."

"Why should I care about that? When did they ever think I did anything right?"

"Henny, we need to stop going to yard sales. I don't feel good about contributing to this any longer."

What? How dare Ida Mae try to threaten her with putting a stop to yard-saling! Henny grew warm, and her breath quickened. Anger oozed over the surface of her shame, like oil on water, and it caught fire. She nudged her sister backward, a little too hard perhaps, and slammed the door shut. "Go back to the kitchen and mind your business."

"Fine. Have it your way. You always do."

Henny sighed. "I'm going to put this shoe away. Will you finish getting our food ready?"

"Sure." Ida Mae huffed, shoving aside a bag of aluminum cans. "I guess we're sitting in the living room to eat?"

"Where else?"

Ida Mae muttered something probably none too kind under her breath.

Henny edged past the piles of books and boxes stacked three feet high, and the bags of empty aluminum cans—she needed to take them to the recycling center—and headed toward the guest bedroom. She tried to open the door, but it caught, not allowing her to enter. Henny pressed harder, but no luck. She shoved against it with her shoulder, and finally it opened enough to allow her to squeeze in sideways. Henny scanned the shelves stuffed with dolls, trinkets, *Wizard of Oz* items, and the loads of clothes, toys, boxes, shoes, pictures, and such heaped on the bed, and on the floor. A narrow path cut through the treasures, revealing gray carpet below.

Henny lifted the shoe to the light, turning it to watch it glitter like rubies, like a genuine treasure. The warm joy lingered as she searched for the perfect place to showcase it.

No room in the jam-packed closet stuffed with baby toys and maternity clothes from when she carried Lydia. She touched her favorite shirt—a yellow flowing chiffon with an empire waist. Grief pushed on the bubble of joy, and she quickly shoved away the thought. She took in the bags, purses, a dress dummy, and boxes of crafts she procured with plans of someday making costumes, or a prom dress for Lydia. The sewing machine sat in the top of the closet, the box still unopened.

"Did you really need that shoe, Henny?"

Walter materialized beside her, wearing his usual farm clothes—a pastel plaid, long-sleeved button-down, the breast pocket laden with a pipe. The tucked-in shirt stretched over a small round paunch hanging over the band of the dark blue jeans sagging on his flat bottom. His green John Deere cap sat askew, tipped to the left. He refused to give up that stupid hat even in death. Just once, she wanted him to come back in the nice gray suit she buried him in. Overall, though, he looked healthy and well-rested. In that respect, at least death treated him gently.

"Lord, have mercy. You shore got quite a collection."

Henny stood between him and the pile, crossing her arms. "That's none of your business," she hissed, trying to keep her voice low.

"It's more my business than yours. You're spending my money."

"No, I'm not. That money is *mine*." She poked herself in the chest, right over her heart.

"Only because you sold my farm."

"*Our* farm. And I needed the money because you left me."

"I died, Henny," he said, raising his voice. Then he muttered,

"Under mysterious circumstances."

"Keep your voice down, and you better not be implying I caused your death. You died and left me!" she shouted, raising her volume to match his.

"Aren't we supposed to be keeping our voices down? And did I say you killed me?"

"Well, if someone killed you, then who?"

"I don't know. It's like I have amnesia. There's a lot I can't remember."

"Ghost amnesia? Is that what I'm hearing?"

"What's so weird about that? It's hard to become a ghost. It does things to you."

"This whole thing is weird. It doesn't get much weirder than a woman standing in her house talking to her husband, who's supposed to be dead."

"Anyway..." Walter pouted. He drew his pipe out of his pocket and cleaned it out with his finger. Nothing fell out of it, though. "My daddy gave me that farm."

"I couldn't work the land by myself. And we don't have anyone to give it to. Besides, you sold off stuff too."

He blew in the pipe bowl and hummed as if he didn't hear her.

"Did you come back from the dead just to argue with me? Don't you have anything better to do? All this time, and you're still going on about this—"

Ida Mae's voice rose behind her. "Henny?"

Henny spun and pushed her glasses up on her nose, locking reality into place. Walter blipped into nothingness.

Ida Mae put one hand on the doorknob and leaned against the jamb. "Who are you talking to?"

"Uh..." Henny's mind raced to grab at an answer to satisfy her sister and remove the befuddled look from her face. "I'm upset because I couldn't find something."

Ida Mae frowned. "It sounded like a conversation."

"Nope. Just me in here." Henny tossed a puzzled face back at her sister. "Who else do you think is in here?" She opened her arms and swiveled at the waist to indicate the absence of other people.

Ida Mae hedged, clearly working through something in her mind. "I *know* I heard you talking as if in a conversation..."

Henny laughed. "I always talk to myself."

"What are you looking for, anyway?"

"A place to put the shoe I found."

"You're obsessed. Now come on, are we going to eat this chicken, or is it going cold?"

"I'm coming." Henny picked her way through the pile, closed the door, and followed Ida Mae to the kitchen.

"You know, our Aunt Iveline was crazy as a bed bug," Ida Mae said.

"Yeah, so?"

"She talked to herself all the time. Entire conversations." Ida Mae handed Henny a plate loaded with fried chicken, mashed potatoes, coleslaw, macaroni and cheese, and biscuits.

"I'm not Aunt Iveline."

5

Henny rinsed the flour off her hands at the kitchen sink and glanced out at the purply-pink dawn.

Walter appeared, sitting at the table, smoking his pipe. "I sure do love your biscuits." A faint scent of cherry tobacco tickled her nose. "Lots of butter and honey. That's good eats."

She popped the biscuits in the oven, made a cup of coffee, and set the bacon to sizzling in the cast-iron skillet. Outside, Khan sounded a frantic alarm as Ida Mae walked toward the house.

Henny didn't remember having plans with her sister. She checked her hummingbird photo calendar hanging on the wall by the fridge. On the Monday block, it said only "Hair at 11."

She wiped her hands on the butt of her cotton shorts and opened the door, greeting Ida Mae. "What are you doing here? Did we have plans?"

"Hello to you too, sunshine. No, we didn't have plans. Aren't I allowed to just come see you?"

Henny hesitated, then shrugged. "Well, all right. Suit yourself. Did you eat breakfast?"

"Not yet."

"Well, come on in and get something then. There's plenty." Henny returned to the stove to poke at the bacon.

Ida Mae, dressed in a pink Gatlinburg T-shirt and denim capris with sandals, smelled of woodsy perfume. Pink lipstick caked her mouth. She held up a plastic bag. "I brought an angel food cake and some fresh strawberries and cream."

"You baked?"

"Lord, no. I bought this from Stella's. You know I can't bake to save my life."

Henny sniffed. "Yeah, I know. Lola Conners told me at church last week how much she enjoyed that blackberry cobbler you made her when she broke her hip."

Ida Mae poured herself a cup of coffee. "It's the thought that counts."

"You know good and well I cooked that cobbler, and you led that poor woman to believe you did."

"You didn't tell her different, did you?" Ida Mae stirred sugar into her coffee.

"No, I didn't want her to know my sister's a liar. But it's a good thing you go to church. Maybe the Lord can save you."

Ida Mae laughed while Henny removed the bacon from the pan, placing the crispy strips on a paper towel.

She then opened the steaming biscuits, laying them flat on the plates, and slathered them in a pool of gravy. She placed a few slices of crispy bacon on the side, picked up her plate and coffee, and walked toward the living room. "You can come on into the living room with me if you want. I like to watch the morning news while I eat my breakfast."

Ida Mae followed close behind. Henny flopped down into her recliner and flipped on the television. Ida Mae balanced her plate on top of a stack of books and disappeared into the kitchen to bring a chair into the living room.

During a commercial, Ida Mae said, "I have an idea. Let's clean up one of your rooms."

"No can do." Henny munched her bacon. "I made a hair appointment at Sassy's today."

"Oh yeah? What time?"

"Eleven."

"I'll go with you. Maybe she can squeeze me in for a trim. My hair is so heavy on the top..." She fingered her floppy gray bangs.

A picture of Jenna flashed onto the TV screen, and Henny leaned forward. "Hush up a minute." She turned up the volume.

The pretty, mocha-skinned anchorwoman said, "Our top story this morning. Plumridge native Jenna Lawson disappeared a week ago, when the twenty-three-year-old drove off in her car, a gold Chevy Cavalier, and vanished into thin air. Jenna's father says her bank account is untouched, and her phone goes to voicemail. Her family fears the worst. The sheriff isn't sure if foul play is involved but asks anyone with information to please come forward."

"Isn't that a shame?" Ida Mae said. "I guess she's officially missing now. Well, you know how these young kids are. They get upset with their family or a boyfriend, and they run off. Maybe it's something like that, and they'll find her somewhere in Indiana or Florida, staying with a friend or relative."

"I don't think so." Henny wiped gravy from her shirt. "She's not the sort of girl to go running off without telling anyone."

"Your head is not screwed on right. You're old enough to know you can't judge people based on how they look, or even how they act sometimes. People you think are good people do crazy things all the time."

"You're meaner than a rattlesnake."

"I am not."

"At any rate..." Henny pushed a stack of papers and empty cola bottles off the end table beside her to create space for her plate of half-eaten food. "You think what you want, but I don't believe Jenna is one of those people who does crazy things. She's a good girl, and somebody did her wrong. I know it. And I'll prove it, if for nothing else than to shut you up."

6

Henny and Ida Mae parked in front of Sassy Styles salon at the strip mall on Mulberry Street. The parking lot held few cars.

"Lord, it's hotter than the devil's bathwater out here."

Ida Mae laughed. "That's your hot flashes." She opened the salon door and was met with a delicious blast of cold air.

The salon, an assembly of black plastic furniture, old hair magazines, and hot pink walls, boasted a tanning booth in the back, and a nail tech behind a screen in the corner. A melange of eucalyptus, cinnamon, and chemicals filled the air. Classic rock music played in the background, and pictures of Dottie's hair creations hung on the walls.

Dottie Chase looked up to beam at them, her scissors in mid-air. "Hey there, ladies. It's so good to see you." Her pink spiked hair stood like a rooster's coxcomb down the center of her head.

Raebelle Downs sat at Dottie's station, white and doughy as a dumpling. "Morning. Y'all doing all right?"

They exchanged the usual pleasantries about surviving the heat and setting up fruits and vegetables for the winter.

Dottie said, "I'm just finishing up with Miss Raebelle here. I'll be right with you."

"Take your time, hon," Henny said, sitting in a wicker chair and selecting a *People* magazine to skim.

Dottie and Raebelle jumped back into their conversation.

"What was I saying?" Dottie said, looking at Raebelle in the mirror. "Oh, yes. My sister and I went to high school with her." With her long, pink, glittery nails, she pulled up a piece of short brown hair and *snip, snip, snipped*. "I'm a few years older though, so I don't really remember her."

"Did y'all know her well?" Raebelle said, brushing hair scraps off her purple cape.

"I think Terra knew her some. Very quiet girl." *Snip, snip.*

"Those quiet ones are always the troublemakers. Wilder than a buck deer, hanging around with that trashy Johnson boy, I hear."

Henny's ears perked. She lowered her magazine. "Are y'all talking about Jenna?"

"Yeah," Dottie said. "I hate it for her family. They must be worried sick."

Henny leaned on the arm of the chair. "I know her. See her all the time at The Pit Stop. Sweet girl."

Raebelle *hmphed*. "I hear she worked at a strip club in Lexington. That's not so sweet, if you ask me."

"Raebelle Downs, that's not right. And it's not possible." Henny tossed aside her magazine.

"Well," Raebelle said, hedging, "I know two things." She stuck one pudgy finger in the air. "One, people do things all the time that other people can't believe." Another pudgy finger sprang up. "And two, that no-good trash, Dustin Johnson, knows where she is."

"I don't know him," Henny said. "What makes you think so?"

"They argued in front of that car shop he works at."

"What shop is that?"

"Spit Shine Detailing. He's probably got her buried somewhere behind the building."

Dottie brushed Raebelle's neck and interrupted. "I'm just going to blow-dry your hair real quick." She started up the blow-dryer, the noise effectively canceling out the conversation.

Raebelle paid and left under Henny's frowning gaze.

Henny settled in the seat, and Dottie ran her nimble fingers through her short, white hair.

"Anything more than a trim today?"

"That's all I need. So I can get these bangs out of my eyes."

The door flew open, sounding the chime. A petite woman with a cherry-red Cleopatra hairstyle stormed in. She wore a purple T-shirt with a white lotus printed on the front, and the words *White Lotus* written above the flower. Her name tag read Sonya.

"What's this?" Sonya waved a paper in the air.

"That's the plumbing bill you owe for busting my toilet, and the toilets of this entire strip," Dottie said, planting her fist on her narrow hip.

"I didn't do anything to your toilets."

"The plumber came this morning." Disgust wrinkled Dottie's features. "He fished a bunch of..." She looked around and whispered, "...*condoms* from the line and said most of them originated from your place." She shuddered visibly. "Every toilet in this strip overflowed with those nasty things."

"Lies. Those must have come from the place before us."

"I don't know. That's not my problem. But you're sure going to pay that bill."

Sonya ripped up the paper. "Who's going to make me?" She tossed the bits in the air and stormed out.

Dottie ran after her and shouted out the door. "If you don't pay that bill, I'll report you. I'll have your business shut down."

Sonya yelled something in return.

Visibly seething, Dottie stormed back into the salon, her face as pink as her spiked hair. "I'm sorry you witnessed that. I need a minute to cool down before I cut your hair, Henny." She shook her whole body and puffed out big breaths, as if about to step into a boxing ring.

"Sure, hon. Take your time."

Ida Mae and Henny exchanged a look. Ida Mae said, "What on earth?"

Dottie stopped shaking off the anger and reached for the giant Jolene's cup on her workstation cabinet. "She's a big old B with an itch. There's been nothing but problems since they opened here. But the toilet is the final straw. Absolute nastiness. I cleaned my bathroom with pure bleach, and everything still feels dirty." She fanned her flushed face with a magazine.

"The plumber really found . . . those . . . you know, those . . . " Henny couldn't even bring herself to say the actual word. "*Things?*"

Dottie grimaced. "Yes, he did."

"That ain't right."

Ida Mae said, "Is it possible they came from the business before, like she claims? What used to be there?"

Dottie fanned herself again. "Most recently, a video store, and a comic book store. The same guy owned both and actually lived in the back. Weird guy, so I suppose it's possible the nasty stuff came from him. But he didn't seem the sort of playboy to entertain that many women."

Ida Mae gasped. "I know the place. Supposedly, they kept a back-room of seedy videos.

"So, it's not completely *im*possible," Henny said.

Dottie thought for a few moments and leaned on her worksta-tion cabinet. "But . . . I don't know...There's something funny going on over there. Every night when I leave, there are strange men hang-ing around, and more semitrucks than normal parked in our lot. A couple of men even propositioned me one night."

"Heavens!" Henny said.

"I told them to get away from me, unless they wanted to walk funny for a while."

Ida Mae chuckled. "What did they say to that?"

"They laughed, hooted at me, and said some gross things, so I took off running, jumped in my car, and got out of there. The next day, I called the landlord, Marshall McConner, to report the White Lotus parlor. He called me hysterical with an overactive imagination but promised to look into it. Fat lot of good that did. I tried calling him again several times since then, but all I get is his voicemail. And he never returns my calls."

"Aren't you afraid . . . ?" Henny asked.

"Sure, I am. I purchased a gun the day after those guys proposi-tioned me, and I got my conceal carry permit. Figure I need something a little stronger than pepper spray to protect myself."

"That's awful. I never thought I'd see the day a young woman couldn't feel safe in Plumridge," Ida Mae said.

"I hear you. This isn't New York City or something." Henny thought of Benson and Stabler from *Law and Order: SVU* chasing a host of criminals through the dark and twisted streets of the giant metropolis.

Dottie snorted. "This ain't Mayberry either. Ain't no one safe anywhere." She stood and turned to check her hair in the mirror. "And if you ask me, I think that place is a brothel."

"No!" Henny and Ida Mae gasped in unison.

Dottie nodded. "Sure do." She put a cape around Henny and snapped it tight against her neck. "Haven't you heard of massage parlors in big cities getting busted for prostitution?"

"But it's a spa."

"So? Massage is one service they offer."

"Surely, that's not happening *here*." Henny shifted in the seat and fanned the cape over her body. "In little old Plumridge?"

Dottie picked up a comb and scissors and spoke to Henny's reflection in the mirror. "And I'll tell you what else. I think that spa is up to no good with Jenna Lawson's disappearance too."

Again in unison, Henny and Ida Mae exclaimed, "What!"

"That's right."

"What makes you say that?" Henny removed her glasses and squinted at the blurry girl in the mirror.

"I didn't want to say anything in front of Raebelle, because you know how she is..."

The two older women nodded. The Mouth of Plumridge.

Dottie spritzed Henny's hair with water and combed out her white locks. "Anyway, I saw Jenna going in there at night."

Henny gasped. "You're kidding me. Are you sure?"

"I'm positive." She pulled a strand of hair between two fingers, and *snip, snip.*

"For how long?" Henny asked.

"I think at least a month, maybe six weeks."

"Did you ever talk to her?"

"Yeah, once. She said she worked there."

That didn't seem right. Why didn't Jenna mention it in their many discussions about Jenna's school and work-life? Henny needed to have a word with that spa lady.

AN HOUR LATER, as they left the salon, Henny tugged on Ida Mae. "Let's stop by that spa real quick. C'mon."

Ida Mae rubbed the back of her neck where Dottie sheared the hair line. "What for?"

"I want to speak to that woman. Maybe I can find out something about Jenna's disappearance. It doesn't seem right."

The pink neon sign in the window of the White Lotus Spa declared they were open for business. Rattan shades covered the windows.

Henny pushed on the door, and they entered a dimly lit foyer. The smell of incense, and soft, fluty music, filled the air.

A short woman wearing a purple uniform shirt stood behind the reception desk. She looked barely eighteen. She eyed Henny and Ida Mae suspiciously.

Henny scratched her neck. She always itched all over after a haircut. "I want to talk to Sonya, please."

The girl looked at the women and shook her head.

"Please. I won't take much of her time. I only want to ask her a few questions."

The girl called over her shoulder, speaking in a foreign language Henny couldn't identify. The red-haired woman came from the back room through a beaded curtain.

"I only want to know if Jenna Lawson worked here," Henny said. "I consider her my daughter."

Sonya pretended she didn't understand.

Henny exchanged a frown with Ida Mae. "I know you understand what I'm saying because at Sassy's an hour ago, your English sounded flawless."

Sonya again pretended she didn't understand.

The door opened behind them. The younger girl dashed away behind the curtain.

Henny and Ida Mae turned to see a pale, middle-aged man of middling height. He resembled a turtle with sagging jowls and a short, beaked nose. He wore khaki pants and a yellow polo shirt under a navy blazer with gold buttons.

"Afternoon, ladies," he drawled.

Henny narrowed her eyes. She knew him, but from where?

Sonya beamed nervously and said in a thick accent, "Hello, Mister McConner."

His mouth pinched into a tight-lipped smile. "What's going on today?"

Sonya called out in a foreign language. A different girl, younger than the other two, popped out and said, "Please." She motioned toward the back.

"Pardon me, ladies. Got to get my massage. My shoulders are so tight after golfing all day yesterday. Don't want any injuries." Marshall chuckled, stepped past the reception counter, and disappeared with the girl.

"Is that your landlord?" Henny asked Sonya.

The woman shrugged and pretended she didn't understand.

"Fine. I'll get answers elsewhere. Then I'm coming back."

"Have a nice day." Sonya said, in clear English.

Fireworks went off in Henny's blood as she and Ida Mae stepped outside. "Those women are hiding something. I just know it. And I'm going to find out what it is."

"I'm all itchy now," Ida Mae muttered, rubbing the back of her neck. "And by the way, how did you become so close to the Lawson girl?"

"What do you mean?"

Ida Mae fanned her T-shirt and reached down the neck to swipe hair bits off her chest. "You said you consider her a daughter. Do you really believe that?"

Henny stepped off the curb and marched toward her car. "Yes, like the daughter Walter and I couldn't have. And more than that, my friend."

Ida Mae followed Henny across the searing heat of the parking lot to the truck. "Well, what are you going to do now?"

They climbed into the truck. The leather, hot from the sun, burned the back of Henny's legs, and the steering wheel fried her fingers. She flipped the air conditioner on high and threw the truck into drive.

"I'll tell you exactly what I'm going to do. I'm going to go see Jenna's boyfriend, that Dustin Johnson boy. Once I find him."

HENNY DROVE INTO the parking lot at the Spit Shine Detailing shop. A few guys hanging around the open garage bay looked at her with curiosity. An old farm truck like hers did not need detailing. She and Ida Mae walked toward the men.

A wiry fellow with a pimply face and skin the color of scorched butter blew cigarette smoke upward. "Afternoon. Can I help y'all?"

The other guys moved back into the garage, pretending to work.

Henny read the name patch on his navy uniform shirt. "Sean, I'm looking for Dustin. Is he here?"

"Nah." He finished his cigarette and tossed it on the ground, stamping it out. "He's off today."

"Do you know if he's at home?" Henny asked.

He shrugged. "Couldn't tell you for sure."

"Okay. Thank you," Henny said, turning to leave. Then she stopped. "I have a question. Is he dating Jenna Lawson? That cute blonde from The Pit Stop?"

"Yeah. As far as I know."

"Do you know for how long?"

He drew the bandana out of his rear pocket and wiped the back of his neck. "Six months or so. She broke up with some other guy to go out with Dustin."

"What other guy?"

"I don't know. Some jerk."

"Dustin's momma is Georgie Johnson, am I right?" Ida Mae asked.

"Yeah. That's right."

"That's what I thought. I know Georgie from way back. Now, seems I heard Dustin still lives with her? Is that true?"

"I'm not sure. I think so." Someone from within called for Sean, so he said, "I gotta go."

Ida Mae whispered behind Henny, "Now what?"

"First, we're going to Jolene's for lunch," said Henny. "Then we're going to swing by Stella's for a consolation cake."

7

Every town possesses a shady troubled side where crime, poverty, and substance abuse are commonplace.

Beyond the railroad tracks on Route 27, the divide in class and status became clear. They passed ramshackle houses with cardboard and plastic sheeting for windows, and sofas on the front porches. Rusted-out vehicles perched on cinder blocks in the front yards, where dogs chained under trees barked and howled. Landscaping looked either wildly overgrown or non-existent. They passed out of Plumridge proper into rural territory, where Franklin County bordered Jefferson County.

Henny and Ida Mae turned left onto Fox Trail Hollow, a narrow, winding, hilly road flanked by deep ditches overgrown with trees and brush.

Henny slowed down as she and Ida Mae scouted for Georgie Johnson's house.

"There it is." Ida Mae pointed. "That tan brick one."

Despite living near the economically depressed area, Georgie's small ranch home sat on a cleanly mowed lawn shaded with two gigantic oaks. Neatly trimmed shrubs lined the front of the house, the shutters looked straight and freshly painted, and the driveway appeared recently paved.

Henny parked the truck and rolled down the windows to cool it off. A small flower garden near the garage greeted them. A bird bath stood between a "Welcome" flag covered in smiling ladybugs and a hummingbird feeder. They walked up the pebbled path bordered with peonies. A pot of mums, covered with a large burlap wreath ornamented with artificial magnolia blossoms, flanked the front door.

Henny rang the doorbell.

Someone inside shouted, "Just a minute!"

A pear-shaped woman, only slightly younger than Henny and Ida Mae, answered the door. A red tank dress revealed a deep farmer's tan, and freckles danced over her perky, sun-kissed face.

Henny said, "Hi there. Mrs. Johnson?"

"Yes?"

"I don't know if you remember us. I'm Henny Wiley, and this is my sister, Ida Mae Puckett. We used to be Peters."

"Oh, yes. My brother, Hank, hung out with your brother, Cash. Am I right?"

"That's right."

Ida Mae toyed with her earring. "If this is a bad time..."

"Oh, not at all," the woman said. "Please come in." She stepped aside. "Pardon the mess. I'm in the middle of setting up some beans for the winter."

Her small home looked immaculate and sparkling and comfortably decorated. The house smelled of lemon cleaner, dryer sheets, and boiling beans.

Ida Mae looked around. "Such a lovely home. So clean and uncluttered." She smirked at Henny.

Henny wanted to pinch Ida Mae's arm black and blue but settled for mentally sticking her tongue out at her sister.

Family photos covered the plain white walls of the living room and a large gray-velvet sectional sat in one corner near the television. Henny and Ida Mae followed Georgie through the room into the kitchen.

"Let me get you some iced tea." Georgie pulled glasses out of cabinets and filled them with ice cubes from the automated ice machine in the fridge. "So, how have y'all been?" She poured the tea.

"Good, thank you," they both said in unison.

She returned the pitcher to the fridge. "It's been forever since we got together."

"Yes, ma'am. How's Hank been?" Ida Mae slid onto a barstool.

"Very well." She tightened her fluffy brown ponytail. "He's still out at the BEM plant, making those appliance parts. He's a supervisor now."

"Is that right?"

"Yes, ma'am. He almost retired five years ago but keeps hanging on. I quit ten years ago and never looked back, but Hank is doing so well. Thank God." She snorted. "I reckon Hank'll die at BEM."

They chuckled.

Ida Mae leaned on the countertop. "I'm glad y'all're doing well."

"And how's your husband?" Georgie asked Ida Mae.

"Oh, Eddie's very well. He's still working for the electric company. He doesn't seem ready to retire any time soon. Though he could."

They smiled in the camaraderie of married women, but then an awkwardness filled the room when they glanced at Henny.

Georgie quickly switched the subject. "So, what brings you by?"

Henny jumped in. "Actually, I asked her to bring me here. I'm terribly sorry to intrude, but I need to speak with your son, Dustin."

Georgie toyed with a potholder. "Sure, I don't mind. Is everything okay?"

Henny wrung her hands. "Well, his girlfriend is missing..."

Georgie's face puckered. "I know. Poor little thing. I hope she comes home soon. Dustin is beside himself. The deputies think he knows something, but he keeps telling them he don't."

"Well, I know Jenna, so I want to talk to him about it."

"Sure. I'll get him. He's in the basement." She went around the side of the fridge and opened a door. "Hey, Dustin, get up here."

"What do you want?" he shouted.

"You have visitors. Get up here."

Dustin stomped up the stairs. He stopped short, blinking at the two old women. His sun-bleached hair brushed his tanned shoulders. He looked more like a beach boy than a boy from rural Kentucky.

"What's up?"

Georgie introduced him to Henny and Ida Mae. "Miss Henny wants to ask you about Jenna."

His dark brows furrowed. "Yeah?"

"Where is she?"

He shrugged his bony shoulders. "Hell if I know." His sharp Adam's apple bobbed up and down as he spoke.

Georgie smacked the back of his head. "You'll keep a civil tongue when you speak to these ladies, or I'll knock it clean out of your mouth."

He shot a side glare at his mom.

Georgie beamed. "Let's all go to the living room where it'll be more comfortable."

They settled onto the sectional. Henny and Ida Mae sat with their backs to the window, facing the blank television, and Georgie and Dustin sat on the section along the adjacent wall.

Henny leaned her elbows on her knees. "When's the last time you saw her?"

"Why?" Dustin pulled a lighter out of his pocket.

Georgie shifted in her seat. "Boy, is that a lighter in your hands? You better not be smoking again, or I'll skin your hide."

Dustin returned the lighter to his pocket.

Henny reiterated her question. "So, when did you last see Jenna?"

He shrugged. "I don't know."

The women all glanced at each other.

"It's really important."

"Boy," Georgie warned, "you're going to help these women out. They're trying to help Jenna's family."

"Isn't that what the sheriff is for?"

"Dustin, don't test me." She slapped his arm. "And sit up straight."

He shifted in his seat, but didn't fully sit up.

"Now, answer the question. I raised you to be respectful of your elders. Quit acting like a brat."

His face turned red.

Georgie leaned forward and whispered to Henny and Ida Mae. "I am so sorry."

Henny waved away Georgie's comment. "Don't worry about it. But Dustin, if you care about Jenna, don't you want her found?"

He relaxed some. "I already talked to the deputies three times. Like I told them, I last saw her the night before she disappeared."

Henny thought about the sort of questions Olivia Benson from *SVU* might ask a perp in the precinct questioning room.

"May I ask what happened that night?"

"We fought, and she stormed out."

Georgie interjected. "She stayed here with Dustin in the basement sometimes. An arrangement your daddy and I did *not* approve of, by the way."

"What did you fight about?" Henny asked.

Dustin said nothing.

His mother responded. "They fought about a lot of things lately. Dustin started liking another girl—"

"Mom." Dustin sat up and glared at her in disbelief. "Stop."

Georgie ignored him. "Jenna showed more interest in getting serious than Dustin did."

"Mom. Stop. It."

"Didn't you tell me Jenna wanted marriage, and you didn't because of some other girl? Casey-what's-her-name?"

"I ain't doing this." Dustin jumped up and started to walk away.

"Get back in here."

"No. You're embarrassing me." He left the room. A moment later, the basement door slammed.

Georgie turned to Henny and Ida Mae. "I'm sorry, ladies. This whole thing with Jenna twisted him up. I don't know *everything*, but they fought about a lot of stuff lately. Something to do with the other girl. I don't think he was serious about her, and probably liked Jenna more, but he's not ready to settle down. He's only twenty."

Heavy steps thudded up the stairs, and the basement door opened. From the kitchen came the noise of ice clinking in a glass and liquid pouring.

Georgie sat back and crossed her legs. "Dustin is wasting his time at that no-good detailing shop that pays pennies. He could do so much better, but he chooses to live in my basement. Not exactly marrying material, is he? I try and try, but I don't know how to get through to him."

Dustin appeared in the entryway. "Are y'all still talking about me?"

"These ladies have questions. They're looking for Jenna. And I'm trying to help them out."

Offering a cautious glance at Dustin, Henny asked Georgie, "How long did he and Jenna date?"

Georgie fiddled with her watch. "Gosh. I guess six or seven months, maybe. Not real long. Is that right, hon?"

Dustin returned to his seat by his mom. "I'm not getting into this."

Olivia Benson always repeated what the perp said to make sure she got the facts straight. Henny followed suit. She directed the question to Georgie. "So, they argued, Jenna got angry, and left?"

Dustin answered for his mom, "Yeah. I tried to call her the next night, but she didn't answer her cell, so I called her dad's line at the house. He seemed worried."

Henny and Ida Mae exchanged a glance.

Henny leaned forward. "Do either of you know if she worked at a place called the White Lotus?"

Georgie frowned. "She worked at The Pit Stop." She looked at Dustin. "Isn't that right?"

Dustin seemed equally confused. Henny and Ida Mae exchanged another glance.

"What's the White Lotus?" Georgie asked.

Ida Mae answered. "It's a spa. I understand they offer lots of services like facials, waxing, and massage."

Dustin set his tea glass on the coffee table, flopped back on the couch, and rubbed his hands down his face like a Munch painting.

Henny scooched forward in her seat. "Dustin, look. I understand you're a private guy, and you don't want strangers poking around in your life. But I hope you understand we're doing this to help Jenna and her family. We're hoping to find her safe and sound, and the only way we can do that is if we have all the right information. We aren't deputies. I'm not working with them. I'm just a friend trying to help. Can you *please* help us? I'll get down on my knees and beg if I can, but I might not get back up again."

Dustin chuckled a bit at that. "Fine, I thought she started messing with her ex-boyfriend again. She said no, but we fought about it."

Silence pressed down on the room.

Then he added, "But her ex is involved in this somehow. I'm not sure how yet, but I know he is."

"Who's her ex?" Georgie asked.

Dustin snarled and spat the name out like a bitter taste on his tongue. "Bruce Dixon. The biggest douche-wad y'all'll ever meet. They dated for a while, wanted to get married and all that, but they didn't because he ended up being abusive. A real d—" He stopped himself. "Jerk." Dustin stood and walked over to the window, the sun washing over him in a golden glow. "I don't even know why he still wanted her, since he's already engaged to somebody else. But he stalks her all the time. Threatens her."

"He sounds like the sort who thinks if he can't have her, nobody will," Ida Mae said.

Dustin pointed at her. "That's right. Exactly like that."

"Did she ever report him?" Henny asked.

"Yeah. Lots of times. She even got a restraining order, but those are useless." He slouched against the window frame. "May as well be written on toilet paper, for all the good they do."

"Oh, Dustin..." Georgie said.

"It's true. That dude broke the restraining order a ton of times. The sheriff couldn't do anything about it because they couldn't catch him in the act."

"Where's this Bruce guy live?" Ida Mae asked.

"Last I heard, I think he's out on Tanbark Court. In those apartments. I don't know which one is his." Dustin balled his fists. "But I wish I did."

Ida Mae nudged her elbow into Henny's arm and tipped her head toward the door. She stood to lead the leaving ceremony, which in the South took a few rounds of farewells, interspersed with conversation, before anyone physically left the premises.

"Well, we should probably go. Don't want to overstay our welcome. We sure appreciate y'all talking with us. I'm real sorry..."

"Oh, crap." Dustin glared out the window.

"What's the matter?" Georgie and Henny craned their necks.

An official SUV from the sheriff's department rolled up into the drive, parking beside Henny's truck.

A young man, probably in his thirties, puffed up with muscles, unfolded from the driver's side, while an even younger woman, who seemed fresh from the police academy, slid out of the passenger's seat.

"What do they want now?" Georgie asked her son.

He jumped back from the window. "To harass me again."

"Calm down. Not necessarily, hon. Maybe they found something."

"I already told them everything I know."

Georgie stepped around Dustin to the front door. "That's fine. We'll get it all figured out." She put her hand on the knob, waiting for the official notice of the doorbell. Georgie lowered her voice to speak in soothing tones to her adult child, patting down the air in front of her as she spoke. "Just take a breath. Calm down. You did nothing wrong, so there's nothing to worry about. Okay?" The doorbell rang, and she waited a beat before opening it. She put on a bright greeting. "Hello there, deputies. So good to see you. C'mon in."

"Is this a bad time?" Deputy Billy asked.

"Not at all. We have visitors, but I think they're about to leave. Do come in. Please. Would you like some tea?" She stepped aside to let them in.

Billy Sykes filled the doorway and the room. Known as a fair and even-tempered officer, many liked him far better than his boss, Sheriff Jack Basham, and rumblings of late rumored Billy might even run for sheriff.

He touched the rim of his deputy hat at Henny and Ida Mae. "No thank you, ma'am, we just ate. Afternoon, ladies."

Deputy Leticia filled the remaining space with a large and queenly presence. Her tan skin pulled tight across sharp cheekbones. She stood slightly behind Billy, unsmiling, her thumbs hooked into her gun belt. She issued a sharp nod by way of greeting. Few wanted to tangle with her.

Billy removed his hat and spoke first to Georgie. "Ma'am, I apologize for interrupting your visit, but this will take only a few moments." He turned to Dustin.

"No. No, no, no, no, no," Dustin snapped. "I answered all y'all's questions a thousand times. You keep asking me the same things over and over. I ain't got nothing new to say. Jenna's missing, and I know nothing about it."

Billy held out a hand. "Calm down, son. We just—"

"No." Dustin's fists tightened until his knuckles turned white. "No. Y'all need to go out, do your jobs, and quit harassing me. I told you everything I know. *Everything.* I also told you who I think might know something. But did you even talk to Bruce Dixon yet? Are y'all even doing anything about it?"

Ida Mae nudged Henny and guided her toward the door. "We need to go."

"Hold on. I want to—"

"Nope." She continued to push Henny toward the door as she spoke to Georgie over Dustin's rant. "I'm sorry, but we need to go. This looks like a family situation. Thank y'all for your hospitality and thank Dustin for us. I hope they find Jenna real soon."

Georgie closed the door behind them. Henny and Ida Mae stepped off the porch and beelined it to the truck. They climbed inside, and Henny cranked the ignition.

Ida Mae buckled her seat belt. "Do you think he did it?"

"Nah." Henny pulled the gear shift into drive and stomped on the gas. "He ain't the killing sort. He's too weak."

"I don't know." Ida Mae looked out her window at Dustin's house. "He's got a temper. And he *did* say they fought. Maybe she pushed him too far. Maybe he snapped and killed her."

Henny headed toward Route 27. She propped her elbow on the window, guiding the wheel with a couple of fingers. "I don't think so."

"Then do you think he's right about Jenna's ex-boyfriend being involved?"

"I don't know, but we're about to find out."

8

Henny and Ida Mae pulled into the parking lot of the Tanbark apartment complex behind the Sprouts grocery store. Still on the north side of town, the dilapidated shotgun houses pressed close together near dirty, graffiti-blitzed buildings.

Ida Mae slid down into the seat. "Oh Lord. I believe you're on a mission to get us killed. I don't want any part of this."

"What are you talking about?"

"I don't even really know the girl. I don't want to be out here, messing around."

Henny removed the keys from the ignition and gaped at Ida Mae, stupefied. "Come with me on this, and then we'll go home."

"What do you think you're doing? Do you think you're Columbo or something? We don't have any business out here, messing around in this . . . " Ida Mae motioned at the apartment building. "This is a matter for the sheriff. Not for two old ladies."

"We're not old! I'm only sixty-five, and you're only sixty-seven."

Ida Mae shouted. "Old enough to be too old for all this! I'm not getting in the middle of this. Dustin already told us this guy abused Jenna and is a stalker. He's clearly unstable. That's not someone I want to mess with."

Henny opened her door. "All we're going to do is ask him some questions. That's it. Then we'll go home."

Ida Mae wavered. "You're assuming he'll let us live so we can go home."

Henny dropped to the pavement. "Oh, c'mon, you big chicken." She made chicken noises. "Bwoooock, bwock, bwock, bwock, bwock . . ."

Ida Mae glared at her. "Oh, that's real mature."

Henny continued making chicken noises, knowing Ida Mae hated to be called a chicken. She closed the door and stepped away from the truck.

The Tanbark Apartments project, part of a Section-8 development the city council attempted back in the nineties, came to a halt with the more popular downtown renovation project proposed by some slick, citified wheeler and dealer out of Louisville. Everyone knew the downtown renovation project meant gentrification but didn't know what to do about it. And a lot of the wealthier people, willing to make the commute to work in the city—and tired of the crime, noise, and bustle of city life—were moving out of Lexington and Louisville. And wealthier people in Plumridge meant higher property taxes, better schools, and nicer homes. A nasty double-edged sword.

An older man in a fisherman's hat, long plaid shorts, and a cabana shirt sat in a golf cart near the apartment building's entrance. He spoke into a walkie-talkie. Gardening equipment poked out of the back of his cart.

Henny approached him as Ida Mae got out of the truck. She waved at him. "Sir! Sir!"

Pink cheeks rounded when he smiled, revealing a perfect set of dentures. He said cheerily, "Hey there. How can I help you, ladies?"

"You look like you work here."

"Sure do. I'm the jack of all trades. Maintenance man, gardener, and all-around problem solver." He laughed.

"I'm looking for Bruce Dixon's apartment," Henny said.

He paused.

"We're his cousins from Florida. We drove a long way to see him."

"Oh yeah? What part?"

Ida Mae, reading Henny's cues, jumped in, "Sarasota."

"Is that right? The Gulf side, isn't it?"

"Yes."

He pushed back his hat. "I just love it down there. Did some deep-sea fishing in Naples. Ended up catching a tiger shark."

They feigned interest while he went on and on about his fishing trip. When he finally paused long enough to take a breath, Henny jumped in. "I'm sorry, but we are in a bit of a hurry. Which apartment did you say Bruce lived in?"

"Apartment 4C. Up the stairs and around the corner on the left, all the way at the end."

They thanked him profusely, and he drove off in his golf cart. They climbed two flights of stairs in the breezeway, turned the corner, and walked down the open passage.

A television blared inside. Henny knocked.

"Hold on," a woman shouted from within. After a few moments, the door snapped open to reveal a taller than average, masculine-looking woman. She wore cut-off shorts, almost as short as underwear, and a Harley-Davidson tank top. A panther tattoo crawled down her left thigh. "Yeah?" she said, curtly, smacking a wad of gum.

She looked Henny and Ida Mae up and down, apparently vexed anyone dared knock on her door.

Henny stepped forward. "Hi, I'm Henny Wiley, and this is my sister, Ida Mae. Might we speak with Bruce Dixon?"

The woman squinted. "He ain't here. Why you want to see Bruce?" She popped her gum between unusually short front teeth.

"I guess you're his..." Henny paused. "Wife?"

"Nawp. Girlfriend."

"For how long?"

The girl sniffed. "What's it to you?"

A photo hung on the wall over the girl's shoulder. It showed her hugging a man with a squarish nose and chin, and dark hair. Bruce Dixon probably.

"I'm a friend of his ex, Jenna Lawson."

The woman stepped out of the apartment, her large, bony feet bare. "You tell that tramp she better back off, or I'll kick her butt all over this town."

How dare she speak that way about Jenna! "Young lady, I'll tell her no such thing. You need to tell Bruce to stop threatening her."

The woman planted her hands on her hips. "Is that what she said? She's lying." She stepped inside, shoved her feet in black rubber flip-flops, and grabbed her car keys. "I'm going over there right now. I'll kick her—"

"Now, hold on a dadgum minute, missy." A sudden mama-bear spirit rose inside Henny on the crest of her own anger. "I'm just trying to have a civil conversation—"

The girl stopped short. "Who do you think you're talking to?"

"I don't know since you're so ill-mannered, you didn't even introduce yourself."

The girl smacked her gum. "My name is Prue. Now I'm going to go kick her butt." She slammed the door shut behind her and started down the passage, her flip-flops echoing in the breezeway.

"Good luck finding her, since she's missing."

Prue stopped. "What're you talking about?"

"Jenna's missing." Henny and Ida Mae caught up to Prue. "That's why I wanted to speak with Bruce, to see if he knows where she is. Her family and friends are worried about her."

Prue broke out into laughter.

"I fail to see what's funny."

She shrugged. "Sounds like someone's done my job for me."

"What a horrible thing to say," Ida Mae said.

"Hey, she's been nothing but a thorn in my side since Bruce and I started dating about six months ago. He broke up with her, and she couldn't take it . . . " Prue flip-flopped back to them. "So, she's followed him around like a lost puppy ever since. She can't get it through her thick head that he don't love her. He loves me."

"You're already living with him?"

Prue looked Henny up and down. "Yeah, so? There a problem with that?"

Henny didn't want to anger this girl any further, or she might stop providing information.

She lifted her hands in surrender. "You're not my daughter. I don't care what you do. I'm just trying to get the facts straight."

"Whatever." Prue brushed past them back toward her apartment. While Henny talked, Prue unlocked the apartment door and stepped inside.

"All I want is to find Jenna. So, if you think Bruce might know where she is—"

"Look, lady, I don't care about Jenna, or what happened to her. I'm glad she's gone. I hope they never find her. Now maybe Bruce and I can have some peace."

She slammed the door in their faces.

"Spiteful hussy," Henny spun to march toward the parking lot. A swirl of emotions and thoughts fogged her mind, making it impossible to think straight.

"I never met anyone so rude in all my life." Ida Mae half-jogged beside her sister.

They closed themselves inside the truck. Henny glared at the building.

Ida Mae looked from Henny to the apartments. "What're you looking at? What're you doing?"

"I'm thinking."

"About what?"

"Wondering if that little witch hurt Jenna."

9

That evening, in her yellow and black plaid flannel pajamas, Henny stood in her living room, listening to the six o'clock news, and searching in vain through a pile of newspapers for a news story about Marshall McConner. She tried to remember the details.

"It's hotter than the ninth circle of Hades in here." She reached up and clicked on the ceiling fan.

Walter sat in the recliner, a soft glow around him. "You should sit and rest."

"I can't rest right now. I need the newspaper story about that McConner man. Can you remember what I did with that paper?"

"Maybe if you cleaned this place up, you might find it."

"Don't you start with me about that. I won't listen to it. And if you plan on nagging me about the house, you can beam yourself out now, Captain Kirk."

Moving to another stack by the couch, she dug through the yellowed and wrinkled pages.

The phone rang.

"Hey. Did you hear about Marjorie Breeding?" Ida Mae asked.

"No. What's the matter?"

"I just got off the phone with Vera Smallwood, and she told me Marjorie broke her leg. She's at home now, recovering."

Marjorie, an elder's wife at the church, also led the Bible study group for older women.

"But she'll be okay?"

"She's fine. But let's take some food to her and Oscar. I'll do a chicken casserole if you make one of those delicious cobblers of yours."

"I can do that, but you know I make more than cobblers. I bake cakes, and pastries, and pies..."

"I know, sassy pants. But everybody likes the cobbler. Let's take it over in the morning before church."

"Alrighty, but the blackberries are out of season, and I don't have many left. I set up twelve jars this summer, and I'm plowing right through them. So don't ask me to make any more."

"Okay, fine. I'll be over in the morning."

Henny hung up with Ida Mae and looked in the fridge for the butter and milk. No butter. "Of course."

She checked the clock on the microwave. Already almost seven in the evening, and already in her PJs for an hour or so, she hesitated, but waiting until morning to make the cobbler seemed a daunting idea. She toyed with the idea of going out in her PJs, but momma taught her to never enter the public sphere not properly attired, unless her life was at stake.

Henny located the garments she wore earlier. She pulled them off the back of the recliner and grudgingly stepped into her people clothes.

She dared to wear the flip-flops conveniently placed by the door. She blasted the heat in the truck to warm her cold toes, and while backing out of the drive, decided to stop off at The Pit Stop. Closer than the grocery store, and a chance to see if anyone had heard from Jenna yet.

A blast of cold air, smelling like ham and produce, hit her when she opened the door. Lucy Anderson leaned on the counter, writing in a notebook. She lifted her chocolate-colored eyes.

"Hey, Miss Henny. How are you doing this evening?"

"Very well. Just came to get some butter. Got to make a cobbler in the morning for a friend."

"Mm-mm. I love me some cobbler. What kind you making?"

"Blackberry. That's the best one, right?"

"Mm-hm. That's right. Though peach is a close second."

"Yes, ma'am." Henny clip-clopped in her sandals through the fluorescent aisles packed with junk foods. At the back of the store, in the corner, sat a refrigerated case full of dairy and other perishable goods. Henny grabbed the butter and carried it to the front counter.

"Have you heard anything from Jenna? I understand she's been missing about a week."

"I sure haven't. It's awful. I know her daddy is super worried."

Henny's hope deflated. "That's too bad. I guess the sheriff has been out here asking questions?"

"Yes, ma'am. They asked us all to come down to the station. I went immediately, but I didn't know nothing to tell them, really. I hope they find her soon, though."

"How long you been working here now, Lucy?"

Lucy scanned the butter. "Oh, about four years."

"Do you know Jenna very well?" Henny read the charge on the register and extracted cash and change from her wallet.

"We aren't best friends, but I know her pretty well. We went to the same high school. And I helped her get a job here..." Lucy looked up as if the answer hung above her head. "We hang out some, but mostly, we run in different circles."

Henny handed the payment to Lucy. "Does she ever talk to you about her personal life, like who she's dating, or anything?"

Lucy completed the sale and dropped the receipt into the bag. "You mean, like that no-good ex-boyfriend of hers?"

"You know about Bruce?"

"I know enough. I think he used to hit her because she came in here once with nasty bruises. And the fact he enjoyed messing around with that ratty Scarlton girl."

"Prue?"

"That's right. So, Jenna got fed up. Then he started stalking her, sitting out there in his car, watching her. He and Prue made phone calls, and that girl came in here to make messes and say mean things to her, threatening her. It got so bad she didn't want to work alone anymore."

With each detail, Henny grew steadily angrier. *Oh, poor Jenna. I let you down.*

"Why did she do it then?"

"We're short-staffed, and she needed the money." Lucy glanced out the window at the gas pump and reached over to push a button. "I don't like it, but that's how it is."

"What about her boyfriend, Dustin?"

"I don't know much about him." Lucy leaned her hip against the counter. "Only met him once or twice, but he seems harmless. Nice, I guess."

Henny nodded. "So, you don't think he hurt her?"

"Pfft. Naw. Not a fly. Now Bruce... He's all kinds of wicked."

"Really?" Sometimes, a single word could open up a treasure trove of information.

"Oh yeah. He's the sort of guy who wanted her, and other women, but then didn't want her to have anyone else, even though they broke up and he moved on. He's crazy jealous."

Henny frowned. "I went by his place today, and his woman Prue answered the door. She's a piece of work."

Lucy laughed. "Whoo. You got that right. Trouble with a capital *P*."

"Do you know where Bruce works now?"

"Last I heard, he works the night shift at the Titan warehouse. I don't know where he finds the energy to work ten, twelve hours, and stalk her too."

"Crazy and wicked always seem to have more energy than level-headed and good folks."

"A-men."

Henny looped the plastic bag on her wrist. "So, when's the last time you saw Jenna?"

"I guess about two weeks ago."

Henny tried to think of what Olivia Benson might ask a witness. *Her demeanor—that's it.* "Do you recall how she acted? Nervous? Scared? Excited?"

"Ms. Henny, you sound like a sheriff's deputy. You working for them now?"

"No." Henny chuckled to ease Lucy's suspicion. "I'm concerned about Jenna is all. I'm just trying to separate rumor and truth."

"Well, she seemed normal to me. In a hurry, maybe running late for something. But not scared or anything."

"She didn't say where she was going, or what she was up to?"

"Didn't talk much about her private life. Every now and then, she might talk a bit about her love life, or her dad's health, but she never went into a lot of details."

A bearded man entered the store with a nod in their direction and walked toward the beer cooler at the back.

"One last question, if you don't mind?"

Lucy leaned on the counter, playing with the end of a braid. "Shoot."

"I heard rumors she took on a second job somewhere. Is that true?"

"Oh, yeah. She works at that spa called White Lotus."

"Is that so?" Henny's excitement grew as she closed in on some vital information.

"Oh, yeah." Her neatly groomed brows shot up. "Her daddy has the beetus, and you know how expensive that insulin is. So, she took another job to help him pay for the medicine."

Chip bags rattled at the back of the store as the man made his way to the front.

"Does she ever talk about what she does there?"

"She said they hired her to clean up the rooms, greet customers, and set appointments. That sort of thing."

The man took his place in line behind Henny, his arms full of chips and beer. "Big Colonels game tonight," he said, smiling. "Getting the essentials."

Henny stepped to the side while Lucy rang up the man's purchase. She didn't want to end the conversation. "Does she enjoy working there?"

Lucy winced, scanning the chips and beer. "I don't know about that. She said it gave her the creeps. I told her to quit, but she said she needed the money too bad." Lucy took the man's money and counted.

"What did she mean about it giving her the creeps?"

She bagged the man's purchase. "I asked her, trying to get her to talk about it, but then a customer came in, and we never finished the conversation." Lucy held the bag out for the man and thanked him. "But I got the feeling there's something real funny going on there."

"Do you know where Jenna lives? I want to check on her family."

"Yeah. I took her home once when her car broke down. Her father lives out on Jefferson Street, in the yellow shotgun house."

"Thank you so much, sugar, for being so helpful." Henny pulled a wadded receipt out of her purse and used the pen on the counter to scribble down her phone number. "If you think of anything else, will you let me know?"

Lucy smiled, her perfect teeth gleaming. "You know I will."

Henny stepped outside and instinctively scanned the parking lot for the yellow car.

She stepped off the curb toward her vehicle, muttering to herself.

"I bet the ex and his hussy are guilty of something." She jerked open her door and slammed it. "I'll tie him to the back of my truck, drive him full speed up to the top of Red River Gorge, and throw him over the side. That's what I'll do. "

Henny jammed the key into the ignition. Of course, Bruce might not have been involved at all. Maybe Prue did something to Jenna. Or who knows—in this crazy world, maybe both of them did it together. Maybe Prue, as the real mastermind, pressed Bruce into doing something he didn't totally want to do. Like Bonnie and Clyde. *Deadly.*

"Oh, Lord, I hope Jenna is safe," Henny prayed. "I can't have another one taken from me."

10

Henny crept down Jefferson Street, squinting in the darkness, searching for a yellow shotgun house. She made a mental note to make an appointment with the eye doctor to discuss her gradually failing night vision, especially unfortunate given her nighttime proclivities for dumpster diving.

Near the end of the cul-de-sac, with a small red maple in the front yard, stood the house. A porch light highlighted the rusty gray vehicle sitting in the driveway.

Henny parked behind the car and climbed the wooden ramp to the door. A TV blared. She peered into the open screen.

"Hello? Anyone there?"

"Hold on." Dishes clattered. A man lurched from the other room with a walker. He grunted as he propelled himself forward. "Yes?" he said, as if it was difficult to breathe. "How can I help you?" His long, grizzled, golden-red beard shifted as he spoke.

"Mr. Lawson? It's me, Henny Wiley. We spoke on the phone about Jenna."

"Oh! Yes, yes. Come on in. It's not locked." Mr. Lawson flopped down in a nearby recliner with a loud sigh. "My dadburned knees are killing me." He set his walker aside and rubbed the offending joints.

The room threw her back into the 1970s. She sat down on the couch—spotted with large brown and orange flowers—in front of a wood-paneled wall covered with prints of pheasants and bird dogs.

Henny pressed her feet into the olive-green shag carpet long ago worn flat.

"Thank you for receiving me. I'm awfully sorry to hear about Jenna disappearing."

Mr. Lawson turned down the TV with a remote. "I miss her something awful."

"Did the sheriff discover anything yet?"

He wiped his eyes on the back of his hand. "Not really. That one deputy—Sykes—he's been out here. He said they talked to her ex-boyfriend, Dustin, who said he didn't know anything. He's a wimp, really. Just some punk kid."

Henny relaxed against the back of the couch. "What about Bruce Dixon?"

Mr. Lawson's face flushed. "That son of a gun needs to be horse-whipped. He put his hands on my daughter once, and I told him if he ever did it again, he should run scared. Of course, I could walk then. I went downhill pretty fast in the past several months."

"Did he ever touch her again?"

"Not that I'm aware of. They broke up, and that's when she started dating Dustin."

"I see. You know, I think Jenna is the sweetest girl ever. I'm so happy to know her." Henny paused, thinking she should extend some goodwill his way. "I lost a daughter not long after birth, and I still miss her terribly."

"I'm sorry for your loss."

"Thank you." Henny quickly switched the subject. "So, tell me more about Bruce."

Mr. Lawson scratched his beard. "It seemed like he put her under some kind of spell, constantly on again, off again."

"Do you think he's responsible for her disappearance?"

"Could be, but I don't know. He came by the night after she went missing, wanting to speak with her. He seemed genuinely surprised to hear she didn't come home."

"Is that so?" Henny looked at the empty Diet Coke cans and bowl of peppermint candies on the coffee table. "That's not at all what I heard."

"What do you mean?"

"For starters, you told me a minute ago, he put his hands on her once." She scooted forward on the couch. "Then I was out at The Pit Stop, and the cashier said he and his current girlfriend harassed Jenna. The way the girl talked, it seemed they stalked Jenna and made her miserable."

"I don't recall Jenna saying anything like that to me."

"I'm sure she didn't want you to worry."

Mr. Lawson slumped in his chair.

Henny's throat tightened. "I'm so sorry to upset you."

He waved away her comment. "No. Don't worry about that. I'm glad I know."

"Bruce must be a fantastic actor," Henny said.

"I suppose it's possible, but he seemed pretty authentic to me."

"Psychopaths are usually pretty good at fooling people."

"You can bet I'm going to lean heavy on the sheriff now to see if I can get them to double down on Bruce, see what they can squeeze out of him. If what you say is true, he *must* know more than he's pretending. I want that boy's skinny neck on a platter." He held his hand up, squeezed it into a tight ball, and growled.

Henny struggled to maintain her calm as her own anger bubbled and fizzed inside her like a shaken soda. As a distraction, she asked for a piece of candy, unwrapped it, and popped it into her mouth. Henny bit into the candy and crunched the sugary shards.

"I just can't believe she's gone. She's all I got. I can't go on without her." Mr. Lawson pulled a napkin off the table by his chair and dabbed his eyes. "Sorry, it's so hard to bear."

His emotion drew out Henny's own tears, and she dug through her purse for a tissue. "Don't apologize. Please. I know what you're going through. It's like a piece of you dies, and you walk around with holes right through your core. Those holes never get filled up either. Believe me, I tried every which way."

He nodded. "They have to find Jenna. They will, right?"

"I'm sure they will. I'm sure they're working as hard and fast as they can."

Mr. Lawson sniffled and looked down at the rumpled napkin he folded between his thick fingers.

"But if Dustin is too meek to hurt her, and you don't think Bruce did it, then who else?" Henny asked.

"I can't imagine."

"Do you know if any of Jenna's friends drive a yellow sports-type car? Blocky front, and on the back the brake lights are three strips on each side."

"Maybe a Mustang? With a black stripe down the hood and a horse medallion on the grill?"

She screwed up her face. "I don't know. Maybe."

"Bruce drives a yellow mustang. Newer model."

"With dark tinted windows?"

He perked like a dog presented with a bone. "Yes. Why? What do you know?"

"The last time I saw Jenna, I saw that car at the convenience store."

Mr. Lawson digested that information. "Did you tell the sheriff yet?"

"No. Not yet."

"You have to tell them, please."

"I will. Right this minute." Henny dismissed herself, wrote down her phone number for Mr. Lawson, and made him promise to call her if he needed anything, or better yet, when Jenna came home.

As Henny climbed into her truck, she noticed a sedan with tinted windows sitting on the side of the road. She heard the engine running. She glanced around the neighborhood, taking in the much less fancy, even dilapidated vehicles. That car did *not* belong here. While the windows hid any discernible features, she could tell someone sat inside.

Henny moved toward the car and called out, "Hey! Let me ask you—"

The vehicle peeled away, far too fast to make out the license plate or model, not that she knew models anyway, but she thought she recognized it as a Mercedes-Benz.

Henny ran back and opened the screen door. "Mr. Lawson, I just saw a dark Mercedes sedan with tinted windows sitting out here, and it took off when I hollered at the driver."

"A Mercedes?" Mr. Lawson pushed himself to his feet and wobbled to the door. He squinted, looking up and down the road. "Who could that be?"

"I don't know. I couldn't identify anything else about it."

"I'm calling the sheriff right now."

Henny followed Mr. Lawson back into the living room. She hovered nearby as he called. He described the vehicle, and she filled in the gaps the best she could when he needed additional information. She listened with anticipation to his "uh-huhs" and "all rights" and "okays."

"Aren't y'all going to send anyone out here?" Mr. Lawson listened for a moment, then said, "Fine, then. That's good enough, I reckon." He hung up without a goodbye, signaling his displeasure. "They said there's nothing really to be done since it's not a crime to park on a street. But they'll send someone to drive through the neighborhood at some point tonight."

"Is that all? And what if they come back and do something to you in the meantime?"

"I guess I'll have to get my gun out. If they won't protect me, I suppose I'll protect myself."

Henny patted his hand. "Is there anything I can do for you before I leave?"

"Nah. I'll be all right."

"Now, don't you worry, Mr. Lawson. I'm going to go down to the sheriff's office this minute and give them a piece of my mind. Maybe I can get them to do something more. Good night."

Henny started up her truck. The clock on the dashboard said eight-thirty already. She glanced at the bag in her seat, knowing she needed to get home and make the cobbler. But after talking to Mr. Lawson, she needed to speak to the sheriff more. The cobbler, and Bruce, could wait a bit longer.

Henny pulled into the sheriff's parking lot. Fluorescent lights lit the windows of the building. As Henny neared the door, she saw a receptionist behind a glass panel, her dark, shiny hair held back tight in a bun.

"May I help you?" the woman said without a smile. Her badge read *R. Hyatt.*

Henny dropped her straw purse on the counter and leaned on it. "My name is Henny Wiley, and I'm here on behalf of Mr. Lawson. What's your name, officer?"

"Rosita."

"Well, Miss Officer Rosita, I'm assuming you spoke with Mr. Lawson earlier tonight?"

"I did."

"I'll have you know, I saw the vehicle. And I'm here to tell you that Mercedes didn't belong in that neighborhood. Mr. Lawson's daughter is missing, and her dad might be in trouble. So, what are we aiming to do about it?"

"As I explained to Mr. Lawson, *we* can't arrest people for being in the wrong neighborhood unless they commit a crime. Maybe the driver got lost."

"No, no, no. I know what I saw. Now, y'all need to get out there and investigate."

"Investigate what, exactly? Is there any damage? Did anyone get hurt?"

That logic took Henny down a couple of notches. "Well, not that I know of, but I'm telling you, something is off."

"You saw a dark Mercedes sedan, right?"

"Right."

"Any plate numbers? A description of the driver?"

"No. I couldn't see any of that. My night vision is awful."

"Right. So, I ask again...what exactly should we investigate?"

Henny tried a different tactic. "What about Bruce Dixon? Did you know he hurt Jenna once? That's proof of a violent temper, right? Maybe he's behind her disappearance?"

"Mrs. Wiley," Rosita said, with forced patience, "I'm sure the officers investigating Miss Lawson's disappearance are doing everything they can. And I'm sure if this Bruce Dixon is involved, they know that, and are acting accordingly. I promise you, we take our jobs very seriously, and our officers are dedicated professionals. Hopefully, Jenna will be found safe and sound and returned promptly to her father."

Rosita's words both reassured and annoyed Henny. "I want to speak to the sheriff this instant."

"Ma'am, the sheriff is not available right now."

Agitated, Henny poked the countertop to emphasize her words. "I'm a taxpaying citizen, and I want to know what you are going to do to help Mr. Lawson tonight."

Rosita glanced down at her desk. "As I informed Mr. Lawson, we will send a patrol through his neighborhood to check on him this evening, but unless there's a crime committed, there's nothing else we can do. There are laws and procedures we must follow."

Henny snatched up her purse. "Fine then. Y'all follow your laws and procedures. I just hope it isn't the death of Mr. Lawson." Henny stormed out of the building, muttering to herself. The logical, but distant and whispering, part of her brain knew Rosita told the truth about laws and procedures. But Henny didn't want to entertain the logical part of her brain. She wanted to believe more could be done. Henny hated feeling powerless.

She flopped onto her truck seat and slammed the door. After starting the engine, she sat for a moment to collect herself. Henny stared at a moth beating itself against a parking lot light and remembered the butter on the seat next to her. She hurried home to make a cobbler.

11

Sunday morning came quickly. Church day, a big day, full of big plans. As Henny outlined her lips in her favorite shade of coral, Walter popped in to sit on the toilet lid. "What are you getting all dolled up for?"

Henny yelped and flinched, running an errant coral mark across her upper lip and nearly into her nostril.

"Dang it, Walter. You made me mess up my liner." She pulled a strip of toilet paper off the roll and wiped the mark away.

"Since when do you look so nice for church?"

"I always try to look nice for church." Henny turned back to the mirror. "You just never noticed."

"Nah. This is different."

She puckered up at the mirror.

"I don't remember you ever wearing so much makeup."

Henny dabbed her lips with tissue and spritzed on some White Diamonds perfume.

"You're even wearing perfume?" Walter jumped to his feet and grabbed for the bottle. His hand passed through her. "Who is he? Who's the man?"

"Go away and leave me alone. You're going to make me late."

"It ain't right." He scowled and vanished.

"You aren't here!" She threw her lipstick into her makeup bag and muttered, "And haven't been for five years. Am I supposed to be alone forever?"

HENNY AND IDA Mae rode together to deliver the cobbler and chicken casserole to Marjorie and Oscar.

They rolled into the church parking lot with only a few minutes to spare. Both women scrambled out of the car and hightailed it to the chapel doors.

Plumridge Christian, a brown stone church dating from 1850, sat in a gently sloping valley in the countryside, only a few miles from Henny's house. The spire jutted from the tops of the ancient pines surrounding the building. Beautiful arched stained glass windows lined its exterior facade.

Henny's heart leapt—and not just from the activity of nearly sprinting to the building. Neville Miller, an elder at the church and one of the most handsome men ever, smiled and shook hands with congregants as they entered the building. His pink golf shirt enriched the glow of his tan. Tall, lean, and silver-haired, he still possessed a strong jawline unmarred by aging.

Neville smiled with cosmetically perfect teeth. He looked like a game show host. "Good morning, Henny. What a pleasure to see you here this morning." His voice, deep and sonorous, made him a perfect baritone in the choir.

Without being obvious, she inhaled his sharp, woodsy cologne. He even smelled good.

"Hey there, Neville. How're you doing?" Ida Mae said behind Henny. She reached across Henny to take a bulletin and nudged her in the back. "Go on. You're holding up the line."

Henny moved forward with a backward glare at Ida Mae.

As they walked toward their favorite pew three rows back from the front, Ida Mae whispered, "Why're you smiling at Neville like a simpleton? I hope you don't have your cap set on him. He's the object of Ruby York's affection."

"Ruby York? Isn't she married?"

The pianist started up, filling the sanctuary with a deep golden melody.

"Nope. Divorced." Ida Mae leaned in and hid behind her bulletin as if the room was full of lip readers. "Not that that ever mattered much to her, I hear."

"That's not my problem." Henny lifted her chin and sashayed to her seat. "Let the best woman win, I say." She shoved Ida Mae to the inside of the pew. "Move down. Go, go."

Ida Mae pushed back, gripping her orange pleather purse close to her body, and slapping at Henny with her free hand. She hissed, "What. Are. You. Doing?"

"Keep going." They sat, and Henny glanced over her shoulder, watching for Neville.

After what seemed like ages, Neville began strolling down the aisle, and Henny noticed Ruby waving him down.

A cloud passed over Henny. She couldn't compete with Ruby's petite figure, those glossy lips. In fact, judging by her toned arms, probably a golfer too. She and Neville could just golf, golf, golf, all the time. He stopped to talk and laugh with Ruby. When he finally glanced up and looked Henny's way, she waved him over.

"Oh, good heavens," Ida Mae whispered behind her. "You're making a fool of yourself. Stop it."

Ruby York slid over to make space for Neville, but he declined, stopped to talk to a few more people on his progress down the aisle, and then hesitated near Henny.

"Hey there, ladies," he said. "So good to see you here. Ida Mae, haven't seen you in a while." His voice seemed teasing and playful.

"I'm here every Sunday," Ida Mae grumbled.

Henny shifted excitedly. "Hey, Neville, we saved you a seat." She patted the empty pew beside her.

"I appreciate it, but I'm sitting up front today. Singing a solo before the sermon."

"Hopefully so low we can't hear you," Ida Mae whispered under her breath.

Henny elbowed her. "Oh, I love to hear you perform. We both do.

Isn't that right, Ida Mae?"

Ida Mae nodded vigorously. "Oh, yes. That's right. We always say how much we love your singing. Why, our congregation is just so lucky to have you."

Henny cut daggers with her eyes to make her shut up. Neville climbed the stairs to sit with the choir, and Henny spent the rest of the service gushing inwardly like a love-washed teenager.

When the service ended, and the ladies exited the church, Ida Mae said, "I sure liked Brother Mark's discussion of Ephesians."

"Uh-huh."

Neville caught up to them. "Hey, Henny."

"Hey," she said. A hot flash waved over her body.

He touched her elbow to stop her, and she flashed a pointed look at Ida Mae.

"I'll wait for you in the truck." Her sister skittered away.

"I won't keep you long." Neville shifted from foot to foot. "Lord, help me, I forgot how nerve-wracking this is."

Henny studied him quizzically, smiling to encourage him.

He touched his shirt collar. "I'm wondering if I might pay a call to you sometime? Or take you out to dinner?"

Her stomach flip-flopped. "Yes, any time," she heard herself say.

Someone called Neville's name. He glanced over his shoulder and waved at a fellow near the church building. "Be right there," he called out. He turned back to Henny. "I need to go help set up the reception hall, but this is great news, and I'll speak with you soon." He winked at her and ran off.

Henny's heart burst into a thousand fluttering butterflies. She practically floated to the truck.

When she didn't start the engine immediately, Ida Mae said, "What's the matter with you?"

"He asked me out. Neville asked to call on me for a date."

"Oh, my! How exciting! When?"

"I don't know. Soon." Henny started the truck.

"Of course, you're going to tell me everything."

"I will." Henny wiggled in her seat and put the truck into gear.

"Don't forget, tomorrow morning, we have the Ladies' Club meeting at the church." Ida Mae checked her lipstick in her sun-visor mirror.

"Mm. Yep."

"What are you going to make?"

Henny shook off her reverie. "Oh, um. I don't know. Haven't thought about it."

"You should make one of your German chocolate cakes. That sucker melts in your mouth."

"Uh, maybe."

Ida Mae closed the sun visor. "Where're we going for lunch today?"

"I need to skip out on lunch today—"

"Are you already going on a diet for Neville?"

"Are you saying I'm fat?"

"No..." She raked her eyes over Henny's figure, actually a little plumper since Walter's death. "I just assumed . . . I mean, if I made a date with a guy I gushed over—"

Henny squawked. "I didn't gush!"

Ida Mae cackled. "You did too!"

"*Any*way..." Henny turned out of the church parking lot. "I'm taking you back to your car because I have an errand to run."

"Why can't we run the errand together? After lunch? I want to go to The Whistle Stop."

The Whistle Stop, a local down-home Southern cooking spot in downtown Plumridge, was nearly impossible to get in on a regular day, but on Sunday, the church crowd flocked there like bees to a daisy as soon as the sermons ended. But Henny found it far more important to speak to Bruce Dixon. Even though Mr. Lawson said Bruce seemed genuinely surprised about Jenna's disappearance, Henny wanted to judge for herself.

"So, what's your errand?" Ida Mae prodded.

"It's something I need to do."

"Why're you being so mysterious? Are you having some illicit affair or something?"

"Of course not." Ida Mae tormented her in only the way a sister could.

"Well? What is it?"

"I'm going out to the Tanbark apartments to see if I can talk to Bruce Dixon."

Ida Mae snorted. "You're out of your mind."

"I only want to talk to him. So I'm going to drop you off, and—"

"Oh, no you don't!" Ida Mae dropped her purse into the floor-board between her legs and shifted in the seat. "I'm going with you in case that fool tries to hurt you."

Henny knew fighting with Ida Mae was a lost cause. Besides, having a little backup, in case she needed it, seemed smart.

As they drove by the Tanbark Apartments, Henny noticed a man getting out of a yellow sports car. She slammed on her brakes, caus-ing the car behind her to honk its horn.

"That's him!"

Ida Mae clutched the handle. "What in hell's fire are you doing?"

"Is that any way to be talking after we just got out of church?"

"Why're you slamming on the brakes like that?"

"That's Bruce Dixon, and his car looks identical to the one out-side The Pit Stop last time I saw Jenna." She whipped into the park-ing lot and plowed toward him.

Ida Mae squealed. "Who do you think you are? Kojak?"

For half a second, an image flashed in her mind of running Bruce down, while shouting, "That's for Jenna Lawson, you creep!"

Henny smiled at the thought of him flat as a pancake, like a car-toon character. Then the sheriff could peel him up with a giant spat-ula.

"Are you crazy, lady?" he said, when she and Ida Mae got out. "You 'bout ran me down."

"I didn't, though." Henny raked her eyes over his lean, but ath-letic, form. A "Fighting Irish" tattoo graced his upper arm.

"You look healthy enough to me," she said.

He pushed his tongue against the wad in his bottom lip, then spit on the asphalt. The glob landed about an inch from her shoe. An image of a sweaty Clint Eastwood in *The Good, the Bad, and the Ugly* flashed across her mind, but she drew in a deep breath, and turned on a moonlight-and-magnolias smile.

"You're Bruce Dixon, aren't you?"

He maintained his dour demeanor but flinched a little. "Yeah, so?"

"I knew it. Jenna always speaks so highly of you. She sure has a spark for you."

He softened, though an air of suspicion clouded his features. "Who are you? Her aunt or something?"

Henny jumped on the lie. "Sure am. On her mother's side."

Ida Mae hovered behind Henny, listening.

Bruce glanced around, clearly confused. "So...what're you doing here?"

"Her father is distraught wondering what happened to his baby girl, and I'm here to see if I can locate her." Henny pretended ignorance of his past with Jenna. "And since you're her boyfriend—"

"I'm not her boyfriend. Not anymore. We broke up."

"Broke up?"

"Yeah, something personal came up, and I ended it with her. Of course, when I told her, she got mad and didn't want to see me again. I'm sure she hates me now. Can't say I blame her."

Henny mentally pushed together some puzzle pieces. Prue and Bruce recently moved in together. Prue seemed emotionally unbalanced. Bruce broke up with Jenna when something personal came up. When she realized the implications, Henny gasped. "Prue's pregnant, isn't she?"

He frowned. "How do you know Prue?"

Henny heaped a healthy dose of sarcasm into her response. "I experienced the pleasure of meeting her yesterday when I came out here to speak with you."

He nodded.

Henny went on. "So, Prue is pregnant, meaning you ended things with Jenna to do the right thing for Prue."

"Yeah, I never wanted it to be that way. Prue and I dated first. We couldn't get along, so we broke up, and I met Jenna soon after." His demeanor softened. "I really wanted to be with her. We even talked about marriage, but not long after Jenna and I started dating, Prue came to me and told me about the pregnancy."

"And you broke it off immediately with Jenna? Her dad said your relationship seemed pretty stormy."

"Yeah." Bruce leaned against his car. "I didn't know what to believe. Prue got around, you know? So, I kept it quiet and continued dating Jenna while I tried to figure out what to do. But Prue is crazy jealous, so she started messing with Jenna."

"What do you mean 'messing with' her?"

He shrugged. "I don't know. Stupid stuff. Following her. Showing up at her work. Prank calls."

"Bullying her."

Bruce looked down at his work boots. "Yeah, I guess so." He pushed at the wad of dip in the bottom of his lip with his tongue.

Henny's stomach lurched as she wondered what Jenna ever saw in this guy. "How long did it go on before you found out about it?"

"A few weeks. I didn't find out until I found Jenna crying in her car. She told me, and I confronted Prue."

"Did she stop?"

"I guess. As far as I could tell. She said the only reason she did it was to scare Jenna off."

Henny glanced around the parking lot. "And that's when you broke up with Jenna?"

"Yeah. I decided to do the right thing by Prue."

"Then why did you always follow Jenna around, threatening her?"

"Who told you that?" He spit away from them.

"I heard rumors."

"Well, they're wrong. I followed Jenna because it killed me that I couldn't have her. I wanted her. I missed her. And trying to give her protection from Prue."

Uncertainty rattled Henny. This seemed to run counter to the rumors about him. "But you hit her, didn't you?"

Bruce held out his hands. "Hold on. I never hit her. I wanted her to quit working at the White Lotus, and she got angry. Said I didn't have any right to tell her what to do. I grabbed her arm, but I swear on a stack of Bibles, I never hit her. There are some creepy characters affiliated with that place, and I just didn't want her going there."

"Like who?"

He scoffed. "I ain't *that* stupid, lady. You trying to get me killed?"

Bruce leaned his forearms on his car to stare across the roof. He kicked at the ground. "Look, I wanted things different. So different. She's all I ever wanted, and I couldn't keep her safe."

"Safe from what?"

"I don't know. She seemed unhappy in general."

"When's the last time you saw her?"

Bruce sighed. "The night you caught me sitting outside the gas station watching her. Before that, I saw her going into the spa one night and I called out to her. But she told me to go away and leave her alone. That's the last time we ever spoke."

"Hey, babe. Whatcha doing?" Prue stood on the sidewalk, her arms crossed over her chest, one leg sticking out. When she noticed Henny, she marched toward them. "What are you doing here? I told you to go away."

Bruce lifted his hand. "Just give us a minute, okay?"

Prue shouted, "She came here before, trying to cause a bunch of problems!"

"She's looking for Jenna!" Bruce shouted back.

"Yeah, I know. I hope they never find her."

"Shut up and go inside."

Prue stuck out her tongue and stormed away.

Henny's brows shot up. "My, my, you two certainly have something solid. She's not even showing yet. Are you sure Prue's pregnant? And are you sure it's yours if she is?"

Bruce started to walk away. "Yeah, we did an ultrasound. Look, I need to go. I'll be listening to this crap all night now."

Henny followed him, and Ida Mae tripped after them. "Hold on, please..."

He stopped, annoyed now. "What?"

"Do you know if Jenna dated anyone else?"

"Yeah. Some punk, Dougie, or something."

"Dustin?"

"Whatever. What she saw in that guy is beyond me."

A door slammed in the distance.

Henny blurted, "Do you think Prue hurt Jenna?"

Bruce stared at her, not angry or shocked, but seriously considering her question. He spit away from them. "She hates Jenna an awful lot, but I doubt it."

Not the same as an unequivocal *no*.

"Did you help her?" Henny surprised herself with her own question.

Ida Mae's head turned slowly to gaze at her with disbelief.

Bruce's dark eyes glinted. "I think that's my cue." He stepped away from the car. "Nice talking to you, ladies. Don't y'all come back now, ya hear?" He walked off.

Henny let him go, watching him stride away.

"I notice he didn't deny it," said Ida Mae.

"Yeah, I noticed that too."

They went back to the truck.

"You think he did something to her?" Ida Mae went around to the passenger side.

"I have no idea. I don't know what to think anymore."

"Now what?"

"We're going to the sheriff's office." Henny peeled out of the Tanbark apartment complex.

She rushed toward the sheriff's department, her mind full of the conversation with Bruce, her skin prickling.

Henny flew down side streets and blew through yellow lights.

Ida Mae gripped the dashboard. "Oh, Lord, help me. Henny, please slow down before you kill us."

When they arrived at the police station, Rosita sat behind the reception window again. She stiffened as Henny and Ida Mae entered the building. "Mrs. Wiley, how may I help you today?"

"I really need to speak to someone right now."

"She meant to say please," Ida Mae interjected, with a gentle push to Henny's shoulder blade.

"I have some important information. Please."

Rosita sighed. "I'll see if someone is available." She picked up the phone and punched in some numbers. "Can you come up front to speak with Mrs. Wiley, please?" A pause. "I'm not exactly sure, but she says it's urgent."

Deputy Leticia opened an inner door.

"Ladies. Good afternoon." The deputy's high cheekbones shone as if kissed with sunlight. "This way, please." She stepped aside to open the door further and pointed down the hall. "Second door on the left, please. Thank you."

Henny and Ida Mae sat at a table inside a room with a mirrored window.

Ida Mae muttered, "Are we getting interrogated or something?"

"Shh."

Leticia pulled out a chair and sat across from the women, her back rigid. She extracted a pen from her shirt and made a note of the day and time on a notepad. "Before we begin, may I get your full names, please?"

Henny and Ida Mae provided the information.

"Thank you. Now, how may I help y'all today?"

"You're one of the deputies working on the Jenna Lawson disappearance, right? We saw you at Dustin's house."

"Yes, ma'am. How can I help you?"

Henny toyed with the handle of her straw purse. "We just came from the Tanbark Apartments where I spoke to Bruce Dixon, and I also recently spoke to Jenna's daddy. Mr. Lawson said Bruce resorted to violence once with Jenna, which I think certainly makes him suspicious."

"Yes, ma'am. We are aware of that history."

"When I spoke with Bruce, he didn't say a thing to make me think he didn't truly love Jenna. He might be innocent."

"Okay." Deputy Leticia's eyes locked onto Henny, her hand

primed to jot down notes.

"He told me his girlfriend, Prue, is full of jealousy and likes to threaten Jenna. I asked if he helped Prue get rid of Jenna, but he never answered my question." Henny stopped, anticipating Deputy Leticia's imminent concern though she didn't seem to pick up what Henny laid down. "Don't you see? He didn't say he *didn't* have anything to do with Jenna's disappearance."

"Right..." Deputy Leticia leaned on the table. "Okay?"

"Did you know Prue is pregnant?" Ida Mae said.

Henny nodded. "That's right."

Leticia seemed to turn something over in her mind. "Uh-huh. Interesting."

Henny continued. "Since Bruce himself said Prue is jealous, and wants Jenna out of the way, the pregnancy probably really put the pressure on Prue to get rid of her rival, don't you think?"

Leticia didn't budge. "Possibly."

"And I saw a yellow sports car at The Pit Stop the night Jenna disappeared." Henny poked the table to emphasize her words. "Bruce Dixon drives a yellow sports car!"

The deputy paused, nodding slowly. "Yes, he does. At this time, however, his alibi seems solid."

"You're going to look into this, aren't you?"

"I will follow up on this information."

"There's something fishy going on with those two, isn't there?"

"I'm not at liberty to divulge the details of our investigation, Mrs. Wiley, but I promise you, we are doing everything we can to find Miss Lawson."

"I'm so worried about her, that's all."

"We certainly appreciate that. We're all worried about her and are doing our best to find her."

"What about the White Lotus Spa?" Henny blurted out.

"What about it?"

"Jenna took a second job there to help pay the bills for her sick daddy. I keep hearing it's not a nice place. A lot of creepy men hang out there."

"Mrs. Wiley, we can't close every business with creepy men for customers. Do you have anything solid?"

"Yes, Sassy's toilet got clogged with condoms, and the plumber says they came from the spa. What about that?"

"Mrs. Wiley, until we receive a valid complaint about the White Lotus, there is nothing we can do."

"Again, with the 'there is nothing we can do' line. Do they teach y'all to say that in training class?"

"Henny!" Ida Mae said. "I'm sorry, ma'am, we're leaving now."

Deputy Leticia stood up. "Is there anything else I can help you with?"

"Not help us with, you mean?"

"Henny Wiley, where are your manners? Come on!" Ida Mae grabbed her sister's purse off the table and threw it at her.

They stood, ready to leave. Henny paused. "Did you hear about the strange Mercedes parked in front of Mr. Lawson's house?"

"Yes, I did." Leticia opened the door for them.

"Guess you're not going to do anything about that either. Well, if I find out anything else, I won't bother letting you know," Henny said.

Deputy Leticia held up her hand. "Mrs. Wiley, hold on. While we appreciate the information, and gladly accept any tips we receive, I must warn you to not insert yourself any further into this investigation."

"But you don't understand. Jenna is one of my favorite people. Like the daughter I lost. I need to know what happened to her."

"I understand, ma'am. However, you must be careful about going too far. If you get in the middle of this, you could not only disrupt what we're doing, but inadvertently damage our case, resulting in obstruction charges. Or worse, put yourself in harm's way."

"I'm only trying to help."

The deputy nodded. "We appreciate your enthusiasm and your willingness to help. But it's for your safety, and ours, as well as protecting the integrity of our case."

"But—"

"Mrs. Wiley, I will not tell you again."

Ida Mae grabbed Henny's arm. "We completely understand. Thank you for your time, officer." She guided Henny away. "C'mon. Time to go home."

When she got in the truck, Henny realized the officer didn't even write anything down, and that fueled her. She didn't care what Deputy Leticia said, or what laws she threatened her with. Jenna needed help, and Henny intended on giving it to her.

12

enny tossed and turned, unable to sleep. She couldn't stop thinking about Neville, or worrying about Jenna, or wondering about the misplaced newspaper with information about Marshall McConner. If Walter loved her like he said he did, he could find it.

And she couldn't stop thinking of that blasted missing shoe. Deep in her gut rose an unsettled, squirmy feeling—a feeling only to be abated by completing the collection.

So, at two o'clock on a chilly morning in October, she slipped into a pair of dark blue jeans, a navy sweatshirt, and gardening boots, and soon found herself at the dumpster behind the Ladybug's Consignment shop. The store sat lifeless, with the windows dark. She needed to work quickly. A mist hovered over the embankment, creating a spooky atmosphere. Crickets chirruped loudly.

She pulled her diving kit from the truck, donned her headlamp, and proceeded with her work. She really wanted to find the mate to the red glittery shoe. Henny pushed up the sleeves of her sweatshirt and launched herself into the bin.

Rustling papers and shifting boxes, she dug through the refuse. "Oh, that's neat." She lifted a small Raggedy Ann doll from under some paper. Some of the yarn hair pulled loose, but she could fix that. Henny dropped the doll inside her pink bag. She found some ribbons, a ripped skirt, and a bow tie—a plaid of pastel blue, yellow, and green. For Neville. Henny tucked it in the bag with the doll.

The sound of squealing tires in the alley scared her, and Henny peeked out the side door just in time to see a dark car rush by. Tinted windows, and only the parking lights on. She clicked off her head-lamp.

The car stopped several yards away at the dumpster behind Sassy Styles. The lack of light reduced everything to shadows, but from her vantage point, it looked like a large, hulking creature got out of the car and moved to the trunk, opening it. Henny squinted. Her feet ached from balancing on her tiptoes on her wobbly crate atop a pile of squished, empty boxes, and her shoulders burned from holding up the lid. The figure seemed to take something from the trunk, but she couldn't make out its shape or size.

"Dang it, I wish I could see better," she whispered to herself.

The shadowy man slid open the side door on the dumpster and shoved the item inside. The figure returned to the trunk and took out what appeared to be bags, throwing them in the dumpster too.

So, someone drove their trash to the dumpster at two in the morning?

Henny's legs shook with the strain, and her shoulder muscles fired. Her balance gave out, and she fell back against a pile of bags and boxes as the lid slammed shut.

"Who's there?" A man's voice called out.

She hunched down in the corner and held her breath, saying a silent prayer for his departure.

"Hey!" the man called again, his voice echoing across the parking lot.

Henny tightened her body into a smaller ball. She listened. If only those stupid crickets would shut up, she might be able to hear something.

Another male voice said, "It's probably just a raccoon. C'mon. Let's go."

Soon, she heard the slam of the car doors, and the vehicle sped away. Henny waited for what seemed like hours. Each minute that passed loosened a muscle until she sat limp and weak. Finally, she stood, stretched, shook out her limbs, turned on the headlamp, climbed out of the dumpster, and gathered her kit.

Henny jumped in her truck and started it up. She stared at the dumpster behind Dottie's salon. Maybe the man threw away something valuable. The squirmy feeling rose in her center, and her palms itched.

Like the lure of the sirens' song, Henny couldn't resist looking inside. She eased her truck up to the bin, left it running, and the door open, in case she needed to make a quick getaway.

Henny unloaded her kit and set up. She noticed several large black garbage bags stuffed full. She reached in and pulled one toward her. She opened it and out spilled a mass of packing peanuts. She checked each bag and found the same contents.

Odd.

Her headlamp lighting her way, she climbed inside the dumpster, and shoved the lighter bags to the side. She noticed another in the bottom, half-concealed under other refuse, as though the man attempted to hide it. Filled with excitement, she grabbed it at the top, planning to jerk it open. But she pulled back when she realized the contents inside felt frozen. She poked it. Sure enough, hard as a stone. A quiet internal voice begged her to run, but curiosity drowned it out. She opened her messenger bag and extracted the box cutter she sometimes used for tough-to-open items. Gently inserting the tip of the blade and holding up the plastic so as not to damage the item, she slipped the box cutter inside and ripped.

Henny gasped and jumped back. A horrid, rotting, almost sickly fruity odor hit her in the face. Retching, she clapped her hand over her mouth and nose, and turned away.

Oh Lord, that's an awful smell. She looked again at the bag, and her heart dropped right into her shoes.

Oh, no. Nonononononono. She sucked in a breath and held it as she ripped the bag all the way open.

A bleachy blonde, wavy-haired girl.

Jenna.

Her blank stare and gray lips conveyed certain death.

Henny's mouth popped open to release a screech. She scrambled out of the dumpster like a rat scratching to safety in a flood, jumped in her truck, slammed the door shut, and locked it. Shaking, she threw her hands over her face and cried.

"Oh, poor Jenna. Poor, sweet girl." Henny opened her glove compartment for a tissue and found only a few restaurant napkins. She sobbed into the wad of napkins as she rifled through her purse for her cell phone. Weeping, and struggling to breathe, she dialed 911.

While she waited for the authorities, her mind swirled with images of the live Jenna, and the dead one. Within a few minutes, lights swept onto the back lot behind Dottie's.

Henny stared at the swirling blue and red colors. They swept over the buildings like a silent discotheque. Deputies Billy and Leticia exited their vehicles and came toward her.

Henny cracked her window.

Deputy Leticia shined a flashlight at her. "Mrs. Wiley? You reported a dead body?"

Henny squinted at the two figures behind it. "Yes, ma'am."

"Can you come out here and talk to us?" Deputy Billy asked, glancing around.

She didn't want to. In fact, she didn't even think she could. Henny felt heavy as a mountain of concrete blocks, and she seemed to hover outside her own body. "Do I have to?"

Leticia rested her hands on her gun belt. "You can sit in your truck, but please open your door."

That sounded safer. "Okay." Her movements seemed heavy and slow, as though she moved through sludge.

Poor Jenna. Poor, poor girl. Her daddy is going to be heartbroken. Henny opened the door and swung around to face the deputies.

"Thank you." Leticia looked Henny over. "Are you all right, ma'am?"

Henny's bottom lip quivered as she tried to stay strong enough to talk to the officers. "I can't believe—" She broke into fresh sobs. "Jenna didn't deserve that."

"The body is Jenna Lawson?"

Henny nodded as she strained against her emotions. "Yes," she squeaked.

"Where is she?"

Henny rubbed her arms, trying to restore feeling in her limbs. "She's in that dumpster right there."

Deputy Leticia told Henny to wait a minute as she and Billy looked in the dumpster. He pulled some crime scene tape from his car and set about marking off the area.

Leticia returned to Henny. She patted Henny's shoulder. "I'm so sorry. I know you felt close to her."

"Yes. I mean, we didn't hang out or anything like that. But I shopped at The Pit Stop all the time. Sometimes I brought her little gifts, and she liked to tell me about school and friends."

"That's nice." Leticia smiled at Henny. Leticia looked pretty when she smiled. "How did you happen to be out here? Diving again?" The smile slipped away, though the warmth remained in her eyes and voice.

The deputies knew Henny liked to hunt for treasures in the local dumpsters, but they tended to look the other way. For some reason, though, this time, Henny felt embarrassed.

"I was."

"Okay. Explain what happened."

Henny related the story.

"Can you describe the car?"

"Not really, it went by too fast. A dark-colored sedan-type car, tinted windows. My eyesight isn't too good at night."

Leticia jotted more notes. "Did you see the driver?"

"No. Just a big blur."

"A man?"

"Yes, because he shouted at me when I slipped and made a noise."

"Did you see anyone with him?"

"Yeah. I heard him speak, but that's it."

"What did he say?"

"When I fell, they heard it, and the guy told the other guy they needed to leave."

"Are you certain the man dumped Jenna?"

"I'm about ninety percent sure he did. He threw in a large package first, then several bags."

"Mrs. Wiley, when you came in yesterday, didn't you mention the dark sedan parked outside of the Lawson home?"

"Yes." Henny perked a little. "That's right. I did."

"The same one?"

Henny squeezed her eyes shut, trying to remember the two cars to compare them. She wanted to be sure. "I think so. Maybe. Could be. It's possible, I guess."

"We'll come back to that."

They went through Henny's statement again. When she finished, the deputy said, "May I see your hands, Mrs. Wiley?"

"Whatever for?"

"I need to check for defensive wounds—cuts, scratches, and the like."

"Do you mean to say you suspect me of hurting Jenna?"

"Mrs. Wiley, this is simply procedure. It looks like we have a murder on our hands now, and I have to make sure this case is completely solid so we can successfully prosecute when we catch the killer."

"But I'm not a killer."

"Ma'am..." Deputy Leticia gathered her patience with a deep inhale and a sigh. "Please, show me your hands." The hard professionalism returned to her voice.

Henny complied, and Leticia shined the flashlight on her hands. She inspected them carefully. "Lift your sleeves."

Henny pulled up the sleeves on her sweatshirt.

"Turn your hands over."

Henny followed the direction. "Satisfied?"

"Yes, ma'am, thank you."

The coroner's van drove up, and the forensics team arrived. They took a ton of photos, removed Jenna from the dumpster, and sealed her in a black body bag.

Emotion and exhaustion drained Henny completely. A stiff gust of wind might blow her over. "May I go home now?"

Deputy Leticia tucked away her pen and notepad. "Of course. But hang around for the next few days in case we need to ask you any additional questions."

13

Henny locked the kitchen door behind her, dropped her treasures on the floor by her shoes, and pressed her head against the cold glass. Her shoulders hung limply.

"What're you doing out so late?"

All at once, she jumped, screamed, and spun around, swinging her striped straw purse through the ghostly form of her late husband. "Dang it, Walter. I told you not to do that."

He chuckled. "You're awake now, aren't you?"

"I don't want to be awake. I want to be asleep, but I can't sleep. That's why I went out."

Walter, wearing flannel pajamas, popped into the corner behind the door. "I see you were out hunting again. Looks like you got some goodies. Anything for Halloween? You haven't even put our decorations up yet."

"With you hanging around, every day is Halloween." Fatigue pressed down on her. "I'm tired. Going to bed." She shuffled toward the living room, her body aching for the nestling buttress of her recliner.

"You stayed gone a long time." Walter materialized in her chair, stretched out, smoking his pipe of course.

She looked at the clock. Five in the morning. "I couldn't help it. I found the missing girl, Jenna Lawson."

"Oh, yeah. I met her earlier."

"Met her? How?"

"When she died. Her spirit left her body, and…"

"Oh, Walter, don't mess with me." She cast off her jeans and sweatshirt, kicking them into a corner against a box.

"I'm not." He puffed on his pipe, little ringlets of smoke floating upward and dissolving. "All us ghosts meet people on their way out."

Henny stood in the middle of the living room in her bra and panties, waving her arms. "Why didn't you tell me that earlier?"

"You went to church."

She snatched her yellow seersucker duster lying on the back of the recliner. "What about when I came home?" She zipped up the duster.

"I didn't have the energy. You think I can just pop in whenever I want? I have to recharge."

"I want to know everything right now. What happened to her? Who killed her? How is she? Does she have any messages for her dad? Or any messages for me?"

"Wait. Hold on—"

"No! I need to know right now. Tell me everything you know!"

"She didn't speak to me. I only saw her for a moment."

"Where did she go?"

"I don't know. Maybe she went to look over someone she loves. Or haunt an enemy." He shrugged.

Henny tapped into her thin reserves of patience. "Okay. Hold on. You said you saw her when she died. Did she die yesterday then?"

He thought for a moment. "No. I don't think so. It was before that."

"Do you not know your days?"

"I'm sorry. I can't help it! I can't remember things properly. Being a ghost does things to you. And my head hurts all the time."

"You can feel pain?"

"Not like you do. It's different."

Henny studied him. Pity softened her annoyance. "I'm sorry for you, hon. I wish you didn't have to go through this. I want you alive again. But please try to think. It's important."

"Ok, maybe two churches ago?"

Henny sighed. "Okay, so I went to church on Wednesday night, so maybe then?"

"Could be."

"Dadgummit, Walter. Get out of here, and go see if you can find her, and get some information about who killed her, and why. I found her body tonight, but someone froze her first, so I'm trying to determine time of death. Please help me out."

"So, now you're a coroner? I'll go later. I wanted to see you."

"But I need to know what happened to Jenna."

"Ain't heard nothin' about her. But I promise, I'll see if I can find her."

"How long do you think it'll take?"

"I don't know. Depends. Our time is different than yours."

"How?"

"Our time goes much faster. One of your days is like a week to us."

"Why?"

"I don't know. It's not like we have ghost school."

"Did you ask?"

"No, I don't care one way or the other."

"Ok, well, if that's all you got, please get out of my chair. I need sleep."

He patted his lap. "Sit right here."

"No, the last time I did that, I shook for hours. And I'm already cold."

"Fine." He popped up to sit on top of the TV.

Henny sat in the recliner and pulled the afghan crocheted by her mother over herself, knocking over a few empty cans onto a stack of magazines. Sleep. Henny desperately wanted to sleep. She yawned. Almost there.

"Your friend is probably trying to wrap up her business before she moves on to her final destination," Walter said, just as Henny nodded off.

She opened her eyes. "Where's that?"

"Not for me to know, darling."

"What good are you, then?" Henny pulled the blanket up around her chin, poked her big toes through the holes in the afghan, and shut her eyes again. "Now, be quiet, and let me sleep. Wait. Why didn't you ever move on to a final destination?"

"My business isn't done."

"What business is that?"

He shrugged. "I'm not sure. I can't remember. I think it has something to do with the pain in my head."

"What do you mean?"

When Walter didn't answer, Henny looked up to find him gone.

A BANGING ON the kitchen door jerked Henny awake. She blinked at the dim gray light of early morning as she struggled against the remnant haze of deep sleep. The banging sounded again.

"All right, all right," she croaked, shutting the recliner footrest. Henny cloaked herself in the blanket and stumbled toward the kitchen. She squinted at the clock on the stove. "Who in their right mind is knocking on my door at seven-thirty in the morning? Better be someone dead or dying."

She peeked through the curtain.

Ida Mae glared at her. "Let me in, eejit."

Henny unlocked the door and turned away, shuffling toward the coffeemaker as Ida Mae let herself in. The air from her sister's entrance sent a chill through the afghan holes, poking at her naked arms and legs. "Close the door," Henny groused.

Henny stared out the window above the sink while she filled the coffee carafe. A thin blanket of fog covered the yard. Khan mercifully didn't report to duty this early, and so didn't sound the alarm of Ida Mae's arrival.

"What in Sam Hill are you doing? It's seven-thirty. And you're not even ready."

"I'm making coffee. What's it look like?" Henny dropped in a filter and filled it with grounds. "Looks like you're already running on high octane." She pulled the blanket tighter around her.

Ida Mae's light floral perfume competed with the coffee. "Uh, hello. The MWC meeting at the church?"

Henny slapped her forehead. "I forgot!" They sat on the holiday committee that put on the Thanksgiving community dinner and the Christmas bazaar each year. "I'm so sorry. I forgot all about it."

"That's just great."

"I'm sorry." The memory of last night flashed through her mind, and she shivered. "I found Jenna Lawson's body in the dumpster behind Dottie's salon." Henny pulled a mug out of the cabinet and filled it with coffee and sweetened hazelnut creamer.

Ida Mae clapped a hand to her chest. "Oh, good gracious, I'm so sorry to hear that." She moved a bag off a kitchen chair and dropped it under the table on top of a pile of books. She sat down. "What happened?"

Henny cupped the hot mug and told her.

"How awful. Poor girl. I hope at least she didn't suffer long. Her family must be devastated."

"As far as I know, her father is her only family, and he's in bad shape. Diabetes."

"So sad all around."

They sat quietly for a while. Henny sipped her coffee. After it worked its beautiful magic, unfurling through her veins and injecting her with the ability to think, Henny broke the silence.

"If you don't care to wait a bit, I can throw myself together, and then maybe we can swing by Stella's for a cake?"

Ida Mae frowned. "It's not as good as your cake, of course, but it'll do. If you think you're up for it."

Henny stormed down the hall, pushing past piles of boxes and bags. After a quick shower, she threw on a pair of olive linen pants, a cream sweater, and brown sandals, and used a setting pomade to muss her hair to match her prickly mood.

When she returned, Ida Mae stood in the center of the kitchen, holding a full garbage bag.

"What are you doing?" Henny rushed forward and grabbed for it.

Ida Mae held the trash out of her reach, and they circled around and around each other. "I'm trying to help you clean up. This place is a disaster."

"It's none of your business. You can't do this. You have no right." Henny made a final lunge and ripped the bag from her busybody sister's grasp. "How dare you touch my things?"

Ida Mae's voice dropped to a serious tone. "Honey, you need help. Big time. Look around. This isn't normal. Humans shouldn't live like this. *No* creature should live like this. Can't you *see* this?" She motioned around the room.

Henny heard only her panic-filled blood *thrum, thrum, thrumming* in her ears. Her mind raced like a weed whacker to shred to bits any thought attempting to form. Panic. Darkness. Fear.

"My treasures," Henny half-whimpered, as she opened the bag and stared inside.

"Treasures?" Ida Mae shouted. "That's trash. Garbage. It's used napkins, and empty cola bottles, and—" She tried another tactic. "Jenna doesn't want this for you."

Henny wagged her finger at her sister. "You hush. You don't know. It's none of your business." Her voice now strained with emotion shrieked, "You have no right going through my things. And don't you dare talk about my Jenna!"

Ida Mae lifted her hands in surrender. "Okay. Okay. Fine. You win."

Walter appeared. He sat on the back of the kitchen chair. "You know, she's right."

Henny snapped her head around to glare at him.

"You don't want to admit it," he said. "I been telling you for years, this is all junk, and needs to go."

"You hush up. Right now. No one needs your input. Go away."

"Who are you talking to?" Fear and concern filled Ida Mae's eyes. She searched the kitchen.

Henny fumbled with the bag. "Uh. You. Who else? Anyway..." Henny swiped her hand through the air as if she could erase this line

Saphia. Fortune Teller. Psychic. Tarot. Palm Readings.

Henny slapped Ida Mae's arm. "Stop the car! Stop the car!"

Ida Mae gasped and slammed on the brakes. "What in the blue blazes?"

Henny pointed at the house now behind them. "Back up and go to that green house."

"A psychic? Really, Henny?" said Ida Mae, when she saw the sign.

"It's worth a try. She might be able to communicate with Jenna. Maybe she can tune in to a clue or something."

"You don't believe in this stuff, do you?"

"No. Maybe. I don't know. I'm willing to try."

Ida Mae and Henny walked up the pebble walkway to the front porch. The door opened.

Miss Saphia couldn't have been over twenty-five, with a fresh, dewy, makeup-free face and bare feet. Between the bracelets on her wrists and the bells on her ankles, she jingled and jangled as she walked.

A silver cat with blue eyes stared from its perch in the window, then licked itself with boredom. A pair of blue parakeets in a cage by the television twittered and fluttered. Plants lined the tops of bookshelves and hung from macramé holders in the corners of the room.

"May I offer you some tea? Or water?"

"No, thank you. I'm Henny Wiley, and this is my sister, Ida Mae Puckett."

"Nice to meet you. How can I help you?"

"I'm here for a reading, I guess."

"Okay. It's thirty dollars for a half hour. What kind of reading do you need? I can do tarot, palm, or sensory perception."

Henny plucked the cash from her wallet and handed it to Miss Saphia.

Ida Mae hissed in a low whisper, "I don't like this, Henny."

As the fortune teller accepted the cash, her eyes flashed on Henny. "You're searching for someone."

Surprised, Henny said, "I found her."

Saphia's frosted blue eyes seemed to peer straight through to the back of Henny's skull. She took Henny's hand. "Your daughter?"

"No." Ida Mae said. "Not even close."

"Well, not exactly . . . " Henny said.

"But close to you."

"Yes."

She gripped Henny's hand harder. "She's dead."

Henny exchanged an astonished glance with Ida Mae. "She is." Her voice shook. "Can you see who hurt her? I want justice."

"A special girl. She's upset. Scared." Miss Saphia closed her eyes. "I see shadows. Darkness. Fear." Her grip tightened around Henny's fingers. "Can't breathe. Cold. Dark." Her eyes popped open. "That's all. I don't see or feel anything else."

"Oh, come on," Ida Mae said. "Thirty dollars for *that*? I could tell you that."

Henny snapped her neck around to stare her sister down. "Now who's the one with the bad manners? If you're going to embarrass me, Ida Mae, you can just wait outside." She waited a beat. "Okay then. I'm terribly sorry, Miss Saphia. Please proceed. Did you see Jenna? Did she tell you what happened?"

"No. I can't see, or speak, to the spirits of those passed on. I only get impressions."

"How?"

Miss Saphia shrugged. "I don't know exactly."

"Did you see how she died? Or who hurt her?"

"No. I didn't see specifics. I'm sorry. Though I did get a distinct male presence right before the darkness, and coldness, settled in."

"So, you think a man killed her?"

"It's possible."

Ida Mae snorted. "Most of the time, when women get murdered, they're killed by men. I mean, I can see that on *Forensic Files*."

Henny glared at Ida Mae.

Ida Mae shrugged. "I'm just saying . . . "

A faint smile lingered on Miss Saphia's lips. "You aren't wrong. Statistically, that's true in domestic situations, while men die at the hands of strangers more often. But that doesn't negate what I sensed."

Ida Mae sighed. "Well—"

Henny said, "Do you know when it happened?"

"Not eight days ago. Not five days ago."

"What in the world does that mean?" Ida Mae asked.

"About six or seven days ago."

Henny's eyes widened. That seemed in line with what Walter alluded to. Maybe she should tell Deputy Leticia. But how to explain a psychic, and a *ghost*, gave her information? Talk about a surefire way to come under suspicion.

Miss Saphia continued. "There's a presence around you. A man."

Henny hesitated. She didn't think Walter could leave the house. "Is he here now?"

"No, but his energy is strong with you. He loves you very much. Maybe a father, a brother, a husband?"

"My husband, probably."

"He's trapped here. You must let him go."

Henny sank back against the sofa arm, confused. She didn't know what to say.

Miss Saphia continued. "He wants to cross to the other side, but there is unfinished business."

"Like what?"

"Something suspicious surrounds his death."

"But the official death is an accident," Ida Mae said.

Miss Saphia ignored her. "He also stays for you."

Henny's back straightened. "I didn't *ask* him to stay!"

Miss Saphia squeezed Henny's hand. "You didn't have to ask."

WHEN HENNY AND Ida Mae returned to her house, Henny told her sister, "You can come in. I'm going to make coffee." She opened the pantry. "And I have these cookies I bought at Stella's the other day."

"I think cookies and coffee will do the trick."

After Henny allowed Ida Mae to clear off the table for a place to eat, they snacked on soft ginger cookies with orange zest icing, and coffee.

"I can help you look for the newspaper." Ida Mae scanned the room. "Though I don't know how anyone could find anything in this place."

"I don't care if you help, but if that's the attitude you're going to have, you can go on home." Henny shoved a chunk of cookie in her mouth. "I have enough to trouble me without you hanging around, harping on me."

"But don't you see how messy . . . " Ida Mae lifted a finger. "No. This is beyond mess. This is a junk heap. A real problem. I'm your sister, and I care about you—"

"I don't want to hear it. It's not like I have roaches!"

"Well, if the bug guy didn't come once a month, then what?"

Henny stared at her sister. She washed the bite of cookie down with coffee and pointed at the kitchen door. "Go. Right now. I don't want you here. I'm tired of listening to you."

14

Henny sat on the couch in her robe, her hair sticking up all over. She positioned herself in the center of stacks of newspapers, listening to the morning news as she sipped her coffee and searched for the article. She'd spent most of the night searching through papers and woke early to resume her hunt.

A pretty anchorwoman with a perfectly coiffed bob said, "Detectives are investigating the death of twenty-three-year-old Jenna Lawson of Plumridge, whose body was discovered in a dumpster early yesterday morning behind Sassy Styles salon."

As the woman spoke, footage from the crime scene flashed on the screen. The reporter on the scene interviewed Deputy Leticia, who never cracked her stony professionalism.

"Do you know her cause of death? Do you suspect foul play?"

"All I can say at this time is that foul play is evident. We do not yet have a confirmed cause of death, but our forensics team is hard at work to determine what happened. We should have a complete picture soon, and we'll proceed accordingly."

"Do you have any suspects?" The reporter stuck the microphone in her face.

Deputy Leticia stood in a military *at ease* stance, with her hands clasped behind her back. "We can't really comment on that, but we can assure the public we are working toward locating and detaining the killer, or killers, as fast as possible."

"There are rumors of a prescription drug issue here in Franklin, and surrounding counties. Do you think Ms. Lawson's death is due to drug or gang activity?"

"It's still very early in the investigation, so we can't rule anything out. I will say we see nothing to indicate that, but again, we still have a lot of work to do to sort this out. Therefore, if you think you know anything, or maybe heard something you think helpful, please give us a call. No tip is too small. Thank you."

Henny sat frozen as she soaked in the news story, and wondered if anyone might call into the tip line.

"What're you doing?" Walter emerged beside her, causing her to jump and splash coffee on the newspaper in her lap. "Clearly not putting up my Halloween decorations."

"*You're* my Halloween decorations. Why don't you go stand in the yard? Can you not warn me before you decide to pop in for these visits?" She folded the paper with one hand and tossed it to the floor on top of the stuffed animals by the coffee table.

"Good morning to you, too, Mrs. Sunshine McGrumpypants."

"I'm not in the mood, Walter. What do you want?" Henny set her cup aside, and picked up another paper.

He reclined on the couch, crossing his feet at the ankles. "What're you looking for?"

"A particular news article about Marshall McConner. If I find the picture, I'll find the article."

"Why's it so important?"

"I can't remember exactly. But it seems like it might somehow connect with Jenna's death. Can you help me look?"

"Nah. Can't pick up paper." He wiggled his fingers. "Not that powerful yet. Maybe someday."

"So, you can move silverware, but can't pick up a paper? Don't you have psychic powers, or insights into the mysteries of the universe, to help me locate the dadburned thing?"

He laughed. "Nope. I don't make the rules. And I don't know any ghosts who can do all that."

"There are others?" She gawked at him.

"Of course there are. If there's *me*, then you know there must be others."

"Huh." She sipped her coffee. "I figured you a figment of my imagination."

"Nope. I'm real."

"How do I know that?"

"Because I told you."

"Who else is over there with you?"

"Over where?"

"Where you are."

"I'm always here."

She rubbed her eyes. "Forget it."

"Look, I'm here all the time, but on a different plane. If you have a glass of water, and you put a stick in it, when you look at it at a particular angle, it looks like the stick is bent, right?"

"I guess. Is this story going to take long?"

"That property is called refraction. It's an optical illusion caused by light rays. That's kind of what's going on here. Most humans see one world. But a few can catch the"—he made air quotes with his fingers—"refraction of light, which helps them see us ghosts. Some days, you're catching the refraction better than others."

"How is it I hear you too? Refraction got anything to do with sound, Mr. Science?"

"No, but . . . look, I don't know everything, okay?"

"So, ask someone who does."

"Fine."

Henny skimmed the pictures of county fairs, beauty queens, the Rotary Club, the library book club. "Anyone else I know captured in the refracted light?" She looked up at him from under her brows.

"We aren't captured."

"You're trapped." She sipped her coffee. "That's what Miss Saphia said."

"Trapped implies I'm here against my will." He pulled his ghost pipe from his pocket and packed it with tobacco. "Who is Miss Saphia?"

"She's a psychic, and she said you can't leave because I won't let you go."

"Maybe I don't want to go because I'm worried about you."

"That's sweet. But I think true happiness waits for you in heaven, don't you?"

"Yes, but..." He puffed on his pipe.

"But you're trapped?"

"No. I think there's something needing resolving."

"What?"

"My death."

"Here we go again with your maybe-I-was-murdered conspiracy theory."

"It's not a theory."

Miss Saphia's declaration tugged at the back of Henny's mind. "Don't you have a guide, or someone to tell you things?"

"Not that I know of."

"Sounds like the spirit world is a lot of work."

"Can be." Walter puffed on his pipe and floated off the couch. He looked like a balloon.

"Any luck finding Jenna?"

"Not yet, but as soon as I meet her, you'll be the first to know." He blew smoke rings. "Horrible what happened to her. You know who did it?"

Henny turned a page. "Lots of ideas. Her ex-boyfriend, Dustin. Her ex-ex-boyfriend, Bruce. Maybe even Bruce's girlfriend, Prue. They're all likely. But the guy who dumped her body is huge. And those three aren't near as big as he is. So, if it is any of them, they didn't work alone."

"What does this ogre look like?"

"I don't know. I only made out the shape of his body in the dark. So, unless he works with one of the three of them, her murderer is someone else entirely. Or he's the killer."

"Hm." Walter stared at the TV screen for a moment, while Henny skimmed another page. "You found the body behind Dottie's, right?"

"Yeah, so?"

"Maybe someone is mad at Dottie. Maybe they're trying to destroy her business. I mean, who in their right mind wants to get beautified where a girl died?"

Henny gaped at Walter. "You know, you might be onto something."

15

Henny stood at the mirror combing her hair when the doorbell rang. She craned her neck to stare down the hall at the clock hanging on the living room wall.

Walter said, "Who's that?"

"I don't know. It's eight in the morning, though."

The neighbor's dog barked its fool-head off.

"They must be out of their mind, coming here at this hour." Walter followed her down the hall.

"What do you care? You're dead. Do you even sleep anymore?"

"It's just the principle of the matter."

Henny put her hand on the front doorknob, the brass cold to the touch. She whispered, "You stay here, and stay quiet. Don't you dare embarrass me, or I'll get someone in here to exorcise you."

Henny peeked out the eyehole. Neville Miller stood on her front porch, wearing khakis and a white polo shirt. "What in the world is *he* doing here?"

She pressed her back to the door, looking down at her attire. Maybe she should change clothes. No, no time.

"Who is it?" Walter asked.

"Neville Miller."

"Aren't you going to let him in?"

The doorbell rang again.

"Heavens, no. Look at this place."

"*Now* you see it? This place is a pigsty. In fact, I don't even think pigs would want to live here."

"Don't you start with me," she hissed. "What am I going to do?" She glanced around, frantic. "I know." Henny wove toward the kitchen through the boxes and bags stacked on the floor. She grabbed her purse and ran back to the front door. "I'll just pretend I'm on my way out now, so I won't be obliged to let him in."

"I don't know why you care, at any rate."

"Hush..." Henny patted the air and opened the door. "Oh, hey, Neville. How are you this morning?"

Walter tried to exit the door behind her, but she closed it through him, effectively turning him into a puff of smoke.

"I hope I'm not interrupting." Neville offered a toothy grin.

"Not at all, but I'm afraid you caught me on my way out."

"Sorry I didn't call first. I'm headed to the golf course and thought to pop over and see you."

"You're headed out awfully early." The dew still glittered on the grass, and Khan still barked in the distance.

He smiled crookedly. "It's never too early to golf. I'd be out there at midnight with a miner's helmet if I could get away with it."

They laughed together.

"Well, I won't keep you since you're leaving. But I wanted to swing by and ask you out before I lost my nerve."

"You lose your nerve over *me*? You flatterer."

He rocked back on his feet. "I'm wondering if you are interested in going to The Red Barn tomorrow night. They have dancing, live music, and some of the best barbeque ever." He shrugged. "Thought it might be fun."

Dancing. Walter never made a spectacle of himself in public. "That sounds like a lovely time."

Henny felt a sharp pain in her scalp. Walter stood beside her, pulling her hair, a look of extreme concentration on his face. She batted at his hand. "Shoo, fly," she said. "Sorry, Neville, please continue."

Neville beamed. "Great. Pick you up at six?"

She flashed a sweet smile up at him. "Thank you for asking. I love the idea of going dancing with you."

"Terrific, see you then."

She waved at Neville from her porch as he pulled out of her drive.

"I don't like him sniffing around here, Henny." Walter sat on the porch swing.

"Good thing it's not up to you. You know, I just realized, I'm going to need a new dress for my *date* tomorrow night."

Walter shot to his ghost-feet, causing the porch swing to rock. "No, you don't. You don't need to buy one more thing. You got a store-full of dresses in the closet with the tags still on them." He seemed to glow brighter, little flares shooting out all around him.

Henny flinched, unsure if the sparks flying at her might burn. "I don't fit in any of those dresses anymore. Besides, they aren't *new* new."

Walter screamed as he vanished.

She shouted into the air, "It's my money too!"

HENNY BARELY SLEPT that night for all the excitement over her upcoming date with Neville. The television flickered, while her mind rolled over the possibilities for the evening. Maybe he might smile at her a certain way. Or touch her a certain way. Or hold her hand. All the things to show he really liked her.

"Hey!" Walter's voice spoke into her ear.

"Ah!" Henny flailed like a turtle on its back. "What in the tarnation are you doing? You scared me clean off my bones."

"I'm sorry. Not trying to scare you," Walter said.

She grabbed up an old newspaper to fan herself. The little clock on the DVD player read 2:00 a.m.

"I met that Jenna girl."

All her anger vanished. "Really? How is she? How did she look?"

"She's wandering in the spirit plane. I guess she's happy because she's surrounded by people who love her."

"What did she say? Did she tell you who killed her?"

"Nope. I introduced myself. She said to tell you hi, and she misses you."

"Oh, bless her."

"She spends most of her time trying to communicate with her father to let him know she's okay. That there's money in a box under her bed. She wants him to use that to pay for his medicine. She saved it for that purpose."

"What else?"

"I asked her if she knows who killed her, and she said no, that someone grabbed her in the parking lot on the way to her car, and a sharp pain entered her arm."

"Like a shot from a needle?"

He shrugged. "She didn't say for sure."

Henny slapped the chair. "Didn't you think to ask?"

"No."

"Oh, this is just like when you went to the doctor. You never asked the right questions."

"Do you want to hear, or not? I didn't come to argue with you."

"Fine. But I don't know why you never think to ask questions."

He floated a few inches off the floor, glowing brighter. "Anyway, the next thing she knew, they put her in a small, dark place, and she felt movement."

"Probably a trunk. Sounds like they grabbed her, drugged her to take the fight out of her, and tossed her in. Did she say where they took her?"

"No."

"And of course, you didn't think to ask."

"She didn't know who did it, or why. Heck, she didn't even know they murdered her!"

"I wonder if there's any way she can find out. I mean, can she go spy at the White Lotus, or something?"

"She's a younger spirit than I am, so her powers are even weaker. It takes a long time to build up any real power to move things, haunt people, and such. That's for the old spirits."

"Okay. I appreciate your help."

"Speaking of power, I'm feeling pretty weak. Got to go, darlin'. Good night."

"Night."

He started to fade.

"Walter?"

"Yeah?"

"Thank you. I really appreciate it, and it's good to know you and Jenna are okay."

"Love you to the moon, Henny." He faded out.

"Love you too."

Henny sat back in her chair and stared at the television, without really watching it.

IN THE MORNING, Henny paid a visit to Miss Saphia. The young woman answered the door in a matching pink tie-dyed yoga top and pants, her hair pulled into a messy topknot. "Mrs. Wiley. How can I help you?"

"I need you to come with me, please. I'll pay you. The young girl who died, the one you consulted me about? She's trying to get a message to her dad. He won't understand if it comes from me. But it can come from you."

"I told you, Mrs. Wiley, I can't actually communicate with the dead. I only receive impressions."

"I know all that. I'll tell you what to say."

Miss Saphia studied her with suspicion.

"I'll explain in the car. Please. I only need an hour of your time, and you'll put a sick old man at ease."

Within twenty minutes, Henny and Miss Saphia showed up at Mr. Lawson's house. He shouted through the screen door, "C'mon in!"

Henny spoke first. "Mr. Lawson, this is Miss Saphia. She's someone who can communicate with the other side. She wants to give you a message from Jenna."

Miss Saphia picked up a frame holding a picture of Jenna in a cap and gown. Her high school graduation. "Your daughter is no longer with us, as you know. But she is watching over you."

Mr. Lawson leaned forward. "Wha—"

"She wants me to tell you she loves you very much. She's with her mother. And they are both watching over you. She says to take your medicine every day."

"How did you know..." His voice trailed off. "Can you see her now? Or speak to her?"

"Unfortunately, no, but I get signals. She says not to worry about her. She's safe. Mostly, she's worried about you. And loves you."

"About me?" His bottom lip quivered.

"She's always been worried about you. I get the impression she wants you to take better care of your health. She misses you."

He wiggled and pushed himself to the edge of his recliner.

"And there's money in a box under her bed for your medicine. She wants you to use that."

Silent tears streamed down his face.

"She believes you have more to do in this life."

"Oh Lord." Mr. Lawson's voice broke. "Miss Saphia, if you ever see my baby girl, or speak with her, please tell her I miss her every day. And I'll do my best to make her proud. I love her always, and I can't wait to see her again."

16

On the way to Sassy Styles and the White Lotus, Henny stopped at a moving sale. She didn't see much she wanted, except a landscape painting of the Red River Gorge, a teddy bear cookie jar—too cute to pass up—and a lamp. But no clothes suitable for a date. So, she moved on to Nicole's Boutique on the downtown square, where she found a pretty chiffon dress of coral and white, a pair of nude heels, and some pearl costume jewelry. She gently laid her purchases on the truck seat next to her.

She passed the Spit Shine Detailing shop. Dustin knelt beside a car, shining the chrome on a mint green classic vehicle of some sort. It looked like something from the fifties, with pointy wings on its tail. Dustin stood and pulled up his drooping pants, which failed to stay up and dropped low on his hips. Henny approached him. He glanced at her, not seeming to recognize her, then did a double take. He resumed his work.

"Hey there, Dustin. Remember me? Henny Wiley?"

"Yeah, uh, sure."

"Can I speak to you in private for a moment?"

He sighed. "Yeah, all right."

They walked over to the soda machine, and he pretended to

study the buttons while glancing around.

"I won't keep you long," Henny assured him, pulling a couple of dollars out of her wallet. "I guess you know about Jenna by now?"

Dustin nodded and looked down at the ground. "I can't believe it, man." He swiped his eyes across the back of his arm.

She handed a dollar to him. "For the machine. My treat. I'm really sorry about what happened to her."

Dustin selected a Sunkist. "Yeah, I'm gonna miss her so much, you know?" He squinted at the sunlight.

"Has the sheriff's office been by to talk to you since finding her?"

"Oh yeah, of course. They're all over me."

"I want to help if I can."

"I don't know how."

"I think if I can figure out who killed her, I can get the deputies to listen to me, and then they'll back off you." Henny hit the Blackberry Kentucky Spice button and collected the can at the bottom of the machine. It released a satisfying hiss when she popped the tab. "Can you think of anyone at all, besides Bruce Dixon, who might want to hurt her? I know she didn't like being a cleaning lady at the spa."

Dustin squinted at her. "Yeah, because they wanted her to give massages."

"What? How do you know that?"

"We broke up in part because of it."

"Why didn't you tell me earlier? You acted surprised when I mentioned a second job."

"I don't know. I don't know you. Besides, the deputies interrupted us last time."

"Fair enough. Did she have a license to give massages?"

Dustin scoffed. "No. She didn't even really want to work there, but needed the extra money, so she took the job to clean the rooms. Something about helping with her dad's medicine, but then they pressured her into doing things she didn't want to do."

Henny frowned, confused. "Like what? If she wasn't licensed, how could they make her do massages?"

"They aren't real particular about that. Some guy there caught a fancy to her and wanted a massage from her. And probably more than that."

"Like what?"

Dustin glared at her pointedly, communicating a silent message.

It dawned on her. "Oh, my." She clapped her hand over her mouth.

"Now you get it. Anyway, she declined." Dustin sipped his soda. "At first." He kicked at a spot on the asphalt.

"At first? You mean she eventually went along with it?" The shock rippled into Henny. She couldn't imagine her sweet Jenna massaging lecherous men who wanted to . . .

Dustin nodded. "Yeah, she did it. She couldn't resist the money."

Henny clasped her throat. "She did . . . *everything*?"

A pained look twisted his features. "I can't be certain. But I think so. After the first time, she started looking for a different part-time job so she could get out of there. But The Pit Stop didn't have any more hours to give her. And you know how hard it is to find work around here."

Henny nodded. "I understand. I wish I knew about all her problems."

Dustin flushed. "I tried, man. I tried." He threw his can at the wall, drawing concerned looks. "Why didn't she listen to me?"

Henny marked Dustin off her suspect list. He truly cared for Jenna. "You can't blame yourself," she offered.

His supervisor shouted at Dustin to get back to work.

Poor Jenna.

HENNY PULLED UP to Sassy's as she finished her Jolene's fries. She scanned the parking lot. Everything seemed normal.

Dottie sat in a salon chair, eating a bagel with one hand while she texted on her phone with the thumb of the other. "Hey, Henny. I don't have an appointment with you today, do I?"

"Oh, no, sweetie. I only want to chat for a bit. I'm surprised they're going to let you open today."

Dottie took a swig of coffee. "I know, but I spoke with the sheriff, and he said as long as no one goes out back, we're fine. So, I have the back door locked tight." She set aside her phone and hooked one arm over the back of the chair. "And thank goodness, too, because I can't afford to lose business for a whole day. It's bad enough I have to go down to the sheriff's office in Berryville during lunch."

Henny sat in a salon chair across from the stylist. "Why do you have to do that?"

"I think they're going to question me about Jenna Lawson."

"Did you see her recently?"

"No, I haven't seen her in ages."

"So, other than that terrible Sonya woman, are you familiar with any of the people who work at the spa?"

"I only met Sonya once, and a couple of the girls. There seems to be a high turnover of workers."

"Really?"

"I'll see one set of girls for a week or two, and then I never see them again. And a whole new bunch of workers, always women, will come in."

"That sounds sketchy, doesn't it?"

"Especially given the disgusting plumbing issue, and all the strange men, it does."

Henny recalled the hulking figure from the dumpster. "Do you remember seeing a huge guy over there?"

Dottie nodded. "Seems there is one guy who's there pretty often. But I don't know his name. I don't know if he works there, or if he's dating one of the girls." She drank her coffee. "He's a pretty big guy."

"Are there ever any women customers?"

"Sure. Lots of them." She licked some cream cheese off her fingers. "Mostly during the day, though."

"Still, it sounds like once the sun goes down—"

Dottie snorted. "Yeah, once the sun goes down, I'm pretty sure that place turns into a den of sin."

"Is there any reason for someone from over there to plant a dead body on your property to either get you in trouble, or to chase away your business?"

Dottie stood and brushed the crumbs off her clothes. "Oh, I'm sure of it. I reported suspicious activity at that place more than once. And then there's that whole plugging up my toilets thing."

"And the sheriff doesn't do anything about it?"

"Every time they come out here, they can't find anything. Everyone's run off, and the place is clean."

"Well, why don't they do surveillance or something?"

Dottie moved to answer the ringing phone. "I don't know, hon. That's a good question."

HENNY STORMED TO her truck, climbed inside, and slammed the door. She dug through her purse, extracting Deputy Leticia's business card from her wallet.

When the officer answered, Henny said, "This is Henny Wiley. Why aren't y'all out here watching the White Lotus? Y'all know there's something bad going on down here, and now with a dead body found—"

"Mrs. Wiley," Deputy Leticia's steely voice cut her off. "I know it can be frustrating, but we have a small department and a small staff. We are aware of reports related to that property, and we're doing everything we can to ensure any criminal activity is dealt with."

"Can't you put surveillance out here, or something?"

"Ma'am, as I explained, we are handling—"

"Grrr." Henny ended the call. She sat for a moment, trying to decide what to do next, when she noticed a woman in a purple shirt with a white lotus on the back. The woman entered the spa.

Well, if the sheriff won't help me, I'll see what I can find out myself. Henny slid out of the truck and marched up to the building. The woman inside looked hardened, with dark hair with frosted spiked tips, and large dark eyes lined in thick black liner. A few light scars lined the right side of her face in a starburst pattern. Henny noticed a small uncolored lotus flower tattoo on the inside of her forearm.

Her name tag said Starla, and she smiled apprehensively at Henny. "How can I help you?"

Henny beamed. "Hello, Starla. I'm Jenna Lawson's friend. I'm hoping to speak with you for a moment."

"About what?"

"I'm just going to speak plainly because I'm tired and upset. My beautiful sweet friend Jenna is dead, and her daddy is sick with grief for her. There are people who believe this place is responsible for her death. I know there are some shady things going on here, things that might be hurting a lot of young women. Might even be hurting you. If something like that is going on here, then I want to put a stop to it, and help young women, like you, who need help."

Starla cleared her throat. She looked around as she pulled a slip of paper from under the counter, jotted something down on it, and said, "Do you want to book a service?" She turned the paper around. It read, Ask for directions to something.

Henny played along, trying to think of something out of the way requiring a lengthy explanation. "Can you tell me how to get to the Newhouse Garden Center, please."

Starla's mouth twitched. "I'm horrible with street names, but I think I can show you." She stepped from behind the counter and rushed to the door. Henny and Starla went outside.

Henny toyed with her truck keys. "Starla, did you know Jenna Lawson?"

"I didn't know her personally because I just got here a couple of days ago." She faked a point down the road to the left and spoke loudly. "If you go this way, and take a right, there's an Arby's there on the corner..." She lowered her voice. "Listen, I don't have long. We need help here."

"You need to speak to the sheriff."

"I can't. They watch us all the time." She spoke loud again to give fake directions.

"Are there others? How many?"

"At least twenty I know, but they split us up. Not all are here."

Henny tried to press Deputy Leticia's business card into Starla's hand.

"I can't. If they find that on me, I'll be next."

"Why don't you run?"

"They watch us constantly with armed guards. We're locked up when we aren't working. They killed the last girl who tried. Maybe that's what happened to Jenna." She raised her voice to add more to her fake directions.

"Come with me," Henny said, craning her neck to see around Starla. "I'll help you get home."

Hope lit Starla's face. "Where are you parked?"

Henny nodded at her truck about fifty yards away. "That white truck to the left."

Starla stiffened like a dog scenting prey. She seemed to calculate something, then having made up her mind, she said, "I hope you can run fast. Let's go." She darted toward the truck, and Henny, completely out of shape, performed her version of what passed for a sprint.

"Hey!" a man shouted behind them.

Henny looked back to see a large guy chasing them.

He passed Henny and caught up to Starla before she reached the truck, cutting her off. The man grabbed Starla's arm and jerked her around. "You can't leave. Your schedule is all booked." He began walking her back toward the building, whispering something to her.

Henny caught up to them. "You let her go right this minute." She pulled out her phone and said, "I'm calling the sheriff. I know what's going on here."

The man grabbed her phone, threw it on the ground, and stomped on it, crushing it beneath his cowboy boot heel.

Henny gasped and picked up her phone. "How dare you?"

The man's head seemed to dip straight into his shoulders.

She tried to match the shadow at the dumpster with the size of this guy. The height seemed right. And hefting Jenna's body by himself looked a breeze.

The man leaned close, his onion breath on her face, and he poked her with a giant finger. "If you know what's good for you, lady, you'll mind your own business."

He needed a nice whack to the head with a shovel. "You let her go."

He resumed walking, pulling Starla along.

"I'll scream," Henny threatened.

"Go ahead."

Henny looked around. There were only a few people outside. By the time she attracted attention, Starla would be gone. And if someone did hear, would they even bother to help?

"Starla, you don't have to do this. Come with me."

"It's too late," Starla said, tears in her eyes. She shouted, "My name is Starla Elliott. I'm from Cincinnati."

"Shut up," the man said, nudging her forward.

They went into the spa where Marshall McConner waited inside. The skin under his chin wiggled as he spoke. "Hello, Rob. Everything okay?" His rheumy eyes drifted around the group.

Henny made a mental note of Rob's first name to tell Deputy Leticia.

"Everything is fine, Mr. McConner," Rob said.

"Good, good. Everything set up for my appointment?"

"Yes, sir."

"Mr. McConner," Henny said, "I want to know why this girl is being held against her will. I want to know what happened to Jenna Lawson."

"That's enough, lady." Rob pushed Henny out the front door and locked it. He smirked at her as she beat on the glass.

"Open this door right now," Henny shouted.

Starla peeked around him. Rob glanced over his shoulder, said something to her, and she disappeared.

Henny pressed her palms against the window.

Rob wiggled his fingers at her mockingly, then turned his back to lean against the door.

"Dang it!" Heart fluttering, and mind in a whirlwind, Henny tried to use her phone, but Rob cracked the glass when he stomped on it, and so she raced back to Dottie's.

Dottie looked up from her haircut. "You're white as a sheet. Are you okay?"

"May I use your phone? Mine's broken."

"Sure, hon. Help yourself."

Henny called the sheriff's department, requesting to speak with Deputy Leticia. When the deputy didn't answer, Henny followed the prompts back to Rosita, the receptionist.

"It's real important you give Leticia this information. There's a big muscular guy who works at the White Lotus Spa. His name is Rob. I don't know for sure if he's the one who disposed of Jenna's body in the dumpster, but he might be. He's about the same size. And he's wicked. He forced this girl to go back into the building against her will. There's something terrible happening at that place."

"Are you sure?"

"Yes. I tried to stop him, but the guy is built like a skyscraper."

"Are you safe?"

"Yes. I'm fine, but I'm worried about her. Her name is Starla Elliott. She says she's from Cincinnati."

"Is he still there?"

"As far as I know."

"Okay. We'll send someone out."

Relief washed over Henny. "Thank you!"

After hanging up with the sheriff's office, Henny ran out to her truck to watch and wait.

About ten minutes later, Sheriff Jack Basham pulled up in front. Henny scrambled from her truck and ran to catch up to him. Waving, she called out, "Sheriff! Sheriff!"

His brown hat sat on a long, almost egg-shaped, head. The skin on his face folded into soft wrinkles like Shar Pei around his sharp eyes and thin mouth.

He screwed up his face. "Yes, ma'am?"

"There's a big guy named Rob in there. He forced a girl named Starla Elliott into the building. She works there, but she wanted to come with me."

"How do you know Starla?"

"I just met her today. She says she's from Cincinnati. But...he put his hands on her. And the rumor is young girls are being forced to work there and give unlicensed massages."

"Who told you that?" Large pockets of purple skin sagged under his eyes.

"Dustin Johnson. The ex-boyfriend of the dead girl found here recently. Jenna Lawson. Dustin says he suspects this place is up to no good."

He nodded. "Okay. I'm going to talk to them. Is this Rob guy armed?"

"I didn't see a weapon, but that doesn't mean anything."

"Okay." He entered the building, and Henny followed him.

A different girl stood behind the counter. She kept a blank face. "May I help you?"

"I'm looking for Rob and Starla," the sheriff said.

The girl glanced at Henny. "There's no one here by those names."

Henny stepped up. "Don't you lie, girl. I saw them come in here myself."

The girl shook her head. "I don't know what you're talking about. There's no one here by those names."

Henny looked at the sheriff. "She's lying. I saw them with my own eyes."

"Do you mind if I look around?"

The girl froze. The manager Henny met before—Sonya, with the red Cleopatra hair—came out from the back room, her face stern. "What is happening?"

Henny leaned against the counter. "Rob forced Starla to come in here. Where are they?"

Sheriff Basham held out a hand. "Mrs. Wiley, please step back."

Henny scowled from behind her buttoned lip.

Sonya crossed her arms over her chest. "What is it you want?"

"I suspect there's a young woman who works here who might be hurt. May I please look around?"

Her dark brows shot up under her bangs. "Who is it you're looking for?"

"Starla Elliott."

Without averting her gaze from the sheriff's face, Sonya shouted, "Starla!"

Starla emerged from the back, her face red.

Henny ran to her side. "Starla, are you okay? You need to come with us right now."

Starla glanced at Sonya. "I can't. I'm working."

"But you know this place isn't safe. Come with me. I'll help you."

Starla extracted herself from Henny. "I-I can't. I have to work."

"Did a man named Rob force you in here?" the sheriff asked.

Starla fidgeted with the hem of her shirt. "No."

"Mrs. Wiley here says she witnessed you being forced inside. If you're in any kind of trouble—"

"I'm not. Rob is my boyfriend." She looked evenly at Henny. "I think Mrs. Wiley is mistaken."

The sheriff planted his hands on his hips. "Young lady, I can't help you if you aren't being honest with me."

"I am."

"No, you're not," Henny cried. "I know what I saw."

Sonya interrupted. "I think we're done here, Sheriff. She answered your questions, and she needs to get back to work."

The sheriff removed a business card from his chest pocket and handed it to Starla. "If you need anything, please call me. My cell is on there. Day or night."

Starla glanced at Sonya before accepting the card. She tucked it into her back pocket. With a quick tip of her chin, Sonya sent Starla to the back room.

Henny turned to Sheriff Basham. "Do something. Please. That girl is in danger."

His jaw tensed. "Ma'am, if you don't mind, I'd like to take a quick look around."

"Go ahead," Sonya said smugly, moving out of the way.

The sheriff stayed gone for what seemed an interminable amount of time. Henny paced back and forth, peeking down the hall. Squeal-

ing tires and a honking horn sounded outside. She peered out the
window to see a white SUV with dark-tinted windows speed by.
Maybe Rob?

As she started to shout out for the sheriff, he reappeared from
the back of the building, and paused near Sonya only long enough to
say, "Thank you for your time." As he passed Henny, he murmured,
"They're gone. I didn't see them anywhere."

Henny followed hard on his heels, stepping out on the sidewalk
toward his cruiser parked along the curb. "I know. I think Rob just
drove off with Starla."

"Are you sure?"

"I can't be one hundred percent certain, because of the tinted
windows."

"What's his description?"

"White. About your height, but beefier, with no neck. Dark goatee and a buzz cut. Thirty years old."

The sheriff opened his car door and sat with one thin leg hanging
out. He picked up his radio mic. "Basham here. 10-6..." He spoke to
Henny. "Did you get a make of a vehicle?"

Flustered, she dithered. "A-a-a white, SUV-type thing with dark
windows. I don't know cars!"

"A Ford? A Chevy?"

Henny ran through the various symbols, the ones she could easily identify. It looked like a fishbowl with a vertical oval in the middle.
"Toyota," she blurted.

"Which way did they go?"

She pointed. "That way. He went right at the light."

The sheriff talked into his radio mic, interspersed with various
codes and lingo incomprehensible to Henny. "Be on the lookout for
a white Toyota SUV, tinted windows, headed south on Boonesboro
Road. Driver suspected armed and dangerous. Female passenger
possibly in danger. Male, six-foot, muscular, about two hundred
pounds, goatee, and buzz cut. Name Rob, no last name identified.
Age approximately thirty. Female. Name Starla Elliott. About five-
five, one-twenty, short dark frosted hair, brown eyes, star-shaped

scar on right cheek, lotus flower tattoo inside left forearm. Over."

A muddled voice answered. How law enforcement personnel understand each other over a radio is anyone's guess.

Sheriff Basham responded, ended his side of the conversation, and hung up the mic. "Got to go. Thanks for your help, Mrs. Wiley. Here's my business card. Any new information, let me know. Bye, now." He shut the door on her before she could say anything else.

Helpless, she watched Sheriff Basham speed away. A car with a loud stereo rolled by and snapped her to attention.

"Oh, shoot! I have a date!"

17

"Neville used to be my friend," Walter said, from outside the shower curtain.

Henny, scalp full of shampoo, stuck her head out. Walter sat on the toilet in a pair of flannel pajama pants and a T-shirt. His black hair, usually combed back in a 1950s James Mae rebel style, looked disheveled.

"Yes, and with any luck, he'll be a friend to me."

"Don't rub it in." He looked up at her with hound-dog eyes. "I can't help it that I'm dead. And you're being so mean about it."

Guilt hit her. "You're right. I'm not trying to be mean. But I hope you understand, I'm lonely."

"You have Ida Mae. And me."

"No. I mean *companionship*."

"So, you're trying to replace me."

"You know that's not possible. You're always number one to me, baby."

"Doesn't feel like it," he pouted.

"Now, go on, hon. I need to get ready. I don't want to be late."

Walter vanished without another word, and the water turned ice cold. Henny shouted at the ceiling, "Stop that this minute!" She waited for the water to return to normal, but it remained cold. "Blast him." Shivering, she quickly finished her shower, then plugged in a space heater to warm the bathroom while she fixed her hair and makeup.

Henny waited on the front porch swing a half an hour before Neville's intended arrival. She didn't want him to see the inside of the house she shared with only the closest people in her social circle, her sister and her dead husband.

The last time she allowed someone else in the house, the look of horror and disgust on the woman's face taught her to be more selective in her acquaintances, and now, they pretended not to know each other at all. Every time Henny saw her at church, or at the Bingo Hall, Henny's face burned with the shameful knowledge the woman likely told many people what she witnessed within the walls of her home.

Henny liked to collect things. Big deal. But even so, hell might freeze over before she invited Neville inside.

Khan signaled Neville's arrival as he pulled up the drive in a gold Nissan Altima. She beamed and waved at him.

Walter leaned against the post.

"Don't you ruin this for me," she muttered through gritted teeth, as she continued to smile.

"I'm not. Don't go out with him, Henny."

She covered her mouth so Neville didn't wonder if she talked to herself. "You just don't want me to be happy."

"That's not true. I hear things about him."

She stood and swiped imaginary dust from her skirt, speaking from the side of her mouth. "Oh, you and Ida Mae. You're both a nuisance, and silly for listening to a bunch of nonsense rumors. And you can't even keep up with what's going on in your world. How can you keep up with mine? Go away."

"Alrighty. Don't say I didn't warn you."

Henny stepped down off the porch as Neville approached with a white rose in a plastic sleeve of water.

"You put this flower to shame. You look so pretty tonight," he said.

Walter appeared behind her. "Wow. He's really laying it on thick. And what a big spender. That rose is from the cash register at The Pit Stop. It probably doesn't even smell good. Not like the roses I grew for you when we owned a *farm*."

Henny ignored the ghost of her late husband. "How sweet of you, Neville. You're quite the charmer."

Neville chuckled and motioned toward his car. "Your carriage awaits, m'lady." He opened the door for her.

"Oh my." She giggled. "I don't remember the last time a man opened a door for me." Henny shot a hard glance at Walter. She also couldn't remember the last time a man made her giggle. Or brought her a rose.

Walter stood on the porch, staring at her with a long face.

THE RED BARN, aptly named and located in the warehouse district in Lexington, took about a thirty-minute drive. Fairy lights wrapped the columns, giving off a soft gold glow. A Southern rock band played on a stage in the covered corner, and picnic tables lined the perimeter of the dance floor under the ceiling fans.

Once inside, the scent of smoked barbeque filled the air. A server girl in jeans, a red gingham shirt, and braided pigtails greeted them at the door, then guided them to a sturdy booth of light oak.

Henny and Neville slid in and took up their menus. After some small talk about their mutual hunger, and what on the menu looked most appetizing, they settled on a shared platter of baby back ribs, hush puppies, corn on the cob, southern green beans, and coleslaw. While they waited for their food, they chatted about the weather, the atmosphere of the restaurant, some of the upcoming events at church, and how they liked the pastor.

Henny's growling stomach turned somersaults when the food finally came. As they each dug into their meals, she realized even though Walter and Neville spent time together through their men's group at church, she didn't really know much about him herself. She started with the basics.

"Have you always lived in Plumridge?"

"No, I'm originally from Illinois."

She bit into a buttery hush puppy. "Oh, I heard you came from Ohio."

Neville sipped his iced tea. "Nope. Chicago, born and raised."

"Any marriages?" She stabbed her green beans.

"Twice, actually."

Henny blinked at the red flag Ida Mae warned her about. She didn't know how to ask more without offending him or appearing too nosy.

As if expecting her questions, he added, "My first wife died in an accident. My second one left me for another man."

Relief washed over her. "I see. I'm sorry to hear that. Sounds like bad luck."

Neville nodded. "Yeah, I guess so."

"May I ask what happened to your first wife?"

He stuffed a bite of coleslaw into his mouth. "One evening, while drinking wine and sitting by the pool, I went inside to open another bottle for us, and to answer a phone call. When I returned, I found her in the pool, facedown." His jaw tensed. "Gone, just gone."

Henny put her hand to her heart. "How awful. Did you have any kids?"

"We chose not to have kids because of our busy careers. We worked all the time, so decided not to bring kids into a situation where they might not get the attention they deserved."

She nodded. "I see." His childless situation somehow seemed sadder than her own. She hoped he didn't ask her about children. Henny felt fragile ever since the incident with Starla, as if her skin, made from the most delicate of glass, might break with the slightest pressure.

But he didn't ask. Instead, he sat back against the booth to continue his story. "The last wife left me in our fifteenth year of marriage. Not the man for her, I guess."

"And you haven't wanted to get married again?"

"I dated a few women, came close once, but ultimately never found the one." Neville beamed his magazine-model smile. "I guess I'm hesitant."

"I understand that. It's difficult to find a good companion."

Dessert in the form of one apple crumble, with vanilla ice cream, arrived with two spoons to share.

"What about you?" he asked. "You ever think of marrying again?" Neville's eyes never left Henny's face. He seemed to look through her as if searching for her secrets.

"No. Walter and I became sweethearts in high school. For the longest time, even thinking about someone else seemed like a betrayal to his memory."

"For the longest time?" Neville cut his spoon into the steaming apple crumble. "Sounds like maybe you don't feel that way anymore."

Henny averted her gaze to her plate and blushed. She picked up her spoon and cut into her dessert. "I don't know. Maybe."

He reached across the table and squeezed her hand. "Maybe there's hope for both of us yet."

Henny stuffed herself so full that merely walking could prove dangerous, so naturally, dancing seemed the way to go.

Neville moved much like a drunken chicken, complete with flapping arms. She struggled not to laugh at him, but his quirky dance-style made him all the more endearing. When he turned his head for a moment, Henny quickly left the rose he gave her behind a potted plant. She didn't dare take it home, as much as she wanted to.

He drove her home and walked her to the door. They stood on the porch under the light for an awkward moment. Khan barked his fool head off, and the still air caused the bark to echo. People in Berryville probably heard him.

Henny knew Neville wanted to be invited in, but Walter obviously planned on quenching that idea when he showed up on the porch swing.

"You're getting home awfully late. Where's the rose?" He started pushing the swing.

Before Walter couldn't pick up a newspaper, but now he was pushing a swing? His ghost batteries clearly ran on jealousy.

Frightened Neville might notice an empty swing moving of its own volition, Henny dashed to it, and sat down. "It's such a lovely night," she said. "I could stay out here all evening." She patted the seat next to her.

Neville sat in what to him looked like an empty spot.

"Hey, buddy," Walter protested. "I'm sitting here."

Neville shuddered. "It's a little cold, don't you think? Maybe we want to go inside for a cup of coffee?" He ran a finger down her arm.

Walter popped onto the porch rail. "Get your hands off her, you bonehead! That's my wife!"

"Oh, how nice, but . . . " Henny couldn't let him see the inside of her home. She needed a fast excuse. "But I need to get up early in the morning. Really early."

"I see."

Walter snapped his fingers. "I guess you expect me to sit here, and watch you fall in love with Neville Miller."

"Sorry I'm not a better dancer," Neville said.

Henny chuckled. "That's okay. I can forgive you for your two left feet."

He pretended to wipe his brow. "Whew!"

"I can't remember the last time I danced. Before I got married . . . " She let her voice trail off, not wanting to implicate Walter of any wrongdoing.

Walter blew in her ear. She brushed him away and looked down at her lap.

"I'd like to invite you in, but the house is such a mess . . . "

"I don't mind. I'll keep my eyes closed." He hooked his finger under her chin and lifted her face. Neville leaned in to kiss her, but she pulled away.

Walter tried to shove his hand between their lips. "Whoa, buddy!"

"Neville, I'm flattered, but I don't kiss on the first date," Henny said.

"How refreshing. I didn't know an old-fashioned woman still existed. In that case . . . " He lifted her hand to his lips and placed a kiss on the back of it.

Henny flushed and stood. "I really should go to bed. Thank you for a lovely time. Good night." She let herself in the door, glancing at him over her shoulder for a last farewell.

He waved. "Good night, Henny."

She stepped inside, closed the door, and leaned against it.

Without a word, Walter flew through the room, generating enough wind to billow her dress and muss her hair. The lights flickered. Newspaper pages separated and floated through the air.

"Walter, cut it out this second. If you keep acting like this, I'm going to move out." An often used, but harmless, threat. Henny couldn't move out, any more than Walter could.

He flew out of the room, leaving the lights on.

"Blast him," she muttered, picking her way through the living room. "It's not my fault he died." Henny grabbed up a sheet of newspaper to make a place to sit. She flopped down, the paper crumpling in her lap. Walter certainly put a damper on her lovely evening. Henny allowed her mind to wander back over the last few hours, to recall the warm feelings Neville brought out in her.

She felt the need for a cup of cocoa. Taking the paper off her lap, she glimpsed a familiar face in one of the grainy black and white images on the front page. Clearly, a younger Marshall McConner.

"This is it! This is the picture!" Henny spoke into the air. "Walter, if you did this, I truly appreciate your help." She waited. "I'm sorry if I hurt you. I'm sorry." Still no response.

Henny flipped the paper around and found the title to the article connected to the image. "Arrested for embezzlement!" She searched for the date. "September 28, 2005." She scanned the article relating the details of an embezzlement case where McConner stole funds from his employer, Hercules Industries, a fracking and mining company. They dropped the charges before trial for a non-disclosed amount. "Sounds like ol' Marshall had the goods on someone."

Henny put on a pair of cozy flannel pajamas and fuzzy socks, and snuggled under her afghan to watch the eleven o'clock news. The top story, about the FBI swooping in to break up a labor trafficking ring at the Gilded Lily restaurant in Louisville, showed tired people, mostly women, stumbling out of the back of the restaurant, squinting at the lights from the camera. Men and women in FBI, ICE, and local law enforcement jackets loaded the people into a van.

Henny sat up on the edge of her recliner, gaping at the television as she watched the report unfold. She knew human trafficking, in a variety of forms, happened all over the world, but never imagined it in Kentucky. Alarms fired off in her head. Louisville, an hour's drive, could be a quick and easy drop-off for Starla. Henny grabbed her phone off the cradle on the nearby table, knocking off an empty soda can and a Cheez-It wrapper. She found Sheriff Basham's business card and called his cell phone from her landline.

He answered, sounding tired, as though sleeping.

"Hi, Sheriff, this is Henny Wiley. We spoke at the White Lotus."

"Yes, ma'am. I remember. How can I help?"

"I'm sorry to wake you, but I just saw a story from the Gilded Lily in Louisville, where they busted open a human trafficking ring."

"Yes?" His voice became alert.

"And I'm wondering if this is related to where they took Starla."

"It's possible. I'll see if I can find out who's leading that investigation. Thank you for your time, Mrs. Wiley, and good night."

"Thank you. Good night." Henny flipped the channel to *Cheers*, snuggled up under her crocheted blanket, and felt the satisfied joy of being helpful.

18

Henny hoped to get to the library to check on Marshall McConner as early as possible, so she could get help from the staff before they became busy with other patrons. But first, she ran by the cellular store to replace the phone that Rob guy smashed at the White Lotus. It took way longer than expected.

Finally, she made her way to the library, a little brown brick building nestled in a cove of trees.

Her new cell phone rang.

"Hello?"

"Hello, pretty lady."

Neville. "Hey there. How are you?"

"I enjoyed myself last night."

Last night seemed like a year ago. "Me too." She smiled into the phone.

"Well, I don't know about you, but I'm ready for some more fun. How's about dinner tonight?"

"Tonight?" She glanced at the clock in her truck.

"Sure, if that's okay. I thought we could watch the Colonels in an exhibition match against Western Kentucky and go to dinner from there."

Nerves wrenched her stomach having to tell Walter about her going to a basketball game. Especially a Colonels one. And to go with Neville? Henny might never hear the end of it.

"That does sound fun. What time?"

"The game begins at five in Lexington. With traffic and parking issues, I'll probably need to pick you up at three."

That didn't give her much time. She could go to the library, or she could go with Neville. Not both.

"You there?"

"Yes, uh, that sounds like a lot of fun."

"Great! I'll pick you up at three."

She raced home and ran inside to shower and slip into a pair of snug jeans and Walter's old blue Colonels sweatshirt, two sizes too big. She took care with her hair and makeup, finishing with a spritz of a light floral scent.

Henny half-expected Walter to appear to challenge her, but he didn't. A hint of cherry tobacco in the air, though, told her he lingered.

She spoke to the ceiling. "Are you still mad at me?"

Silence.

"Are you ever going to talk to me again?"

Silence, but the tobacco scent strengthened.

"Well, I'm going out with Neville tonight, in case you're wondering. I'll try not to be too late."

HENNY NEVER MUCH appreciated sports. It's not that she didn't value the hard work and discipline involved in creating strong, agile players. She just didn't *care*. But she didn't have to care. Being with Neville, being near him in the arena, taking in the scent of his freshly sweet cologne—when she could catch it through the scent of beer and nachos, satisfied her to her core.

As long as he held her hand, Henny wanted nothing more than to sit in the supremely uncomfortable seat, a bag of sticky pink cotton candy in her lap, and content as a puppy with a new toy.

After the game, they returned to the car. The sunset cast the horizon in a purple-gray, and the coolness of the October evening settled in around them. Holding hands, arms swinging playfully, they passed under streetlights in the parking lot.

Neville said, "I'm famished. How about some dinner?"

"That sounds great. What are you in the mood for?"

"I like The Old Mill. They have the best garlic cheese bread."

A cool hollowness opened in her chest. She loved the food, but Henny and Walter enjoyed their fortieth anniversary dinner there. Their last anniversary dinner, actually. She didn't want to hurt her chances with Neville though, so she simply smiled. "That sounds great."

The Old Mill sat in Midway, between Plumridge and Lexington, on a rushing creek spilling into a lake. The restaurant inhabited a rustic restored mill made of gray stone harkening back to the late 1700s. A large wooden wheel dipped its paddles as it rolled slowly, hypnotically, into the water. Inside felt warm and cozy, with a stone fireplace at the heart of the room, and thick barn beams in the ceiling. They sat near the fireplace.

Neville ordered a whiskey sour, and Henny a blackberry spritzer, while they pored over the menu.

Henny couldn't decide between the crab cakes and rice, or the lobster bisque and apple pecan salad. "You're retired, aren't you?" she asked, while deciding.

"I am." He gazed down his nose at the menu. "As are you?"

"Yes. From the library at the elementary school."

"Is that so?"

Someone placed a basket of hot, buttery, cheesy garlic bread on their table. Henny served Neville a slice on a small plate, then served herself. "Oh yes, for forty years. I landed the job just after..." She paused. Mentioning Walter in front of Neville seemed like a betrayal.

"Just after what?"

Maybe if she blurted it, they could move on as though never said.

"After I married. I retired when Walter died." Henny looked down at the menu, her throat getting tight. Before he could say anything, she added, "And what did you do?"

"I owned a carpet and tile company. When my marriage failed, I sold the company, moved down here, and the rest is history, as they say. You know, I think the surf-n-turf sounds great. What are you going to have?"

The lobster bisque went down like sludge. Five years ago, Henny sat in this restaurant with her husband, her high school sweetheart, the only man she ever knew, or loved, or cared about. And now here, a mere month before their forty-fifth anniversary, she shared a meal with another man. Another man she liked a lot.

Neville stopped mid-sentence in his discussion of some TV show. He wiped his lips on his napkin. "Is the bisque not good? You want something else?"

Honestly, she couldn't remember what the bisque tasted like. "Oh, it's lovely," she lied. "I-I-I guess I'm getting full already."

"You hardly touched it. Or your salad."

She forced a smile. "I filled up on candy at the game. I'll get a to-go box."

"What about dessert? They have an amazing chocolate mousse here. The tiramisu isn't too shabby either."

"No, far too much sugar already."

He studied her for a moment. "Did I do something wrong, Henny?"

"Not at all. Truly. Please, continue telling me about the show. It sounds interesting." Some cowboy serial called *The Ranch* on Netflix she didn't give two hoots about. Walter loved westerns though. Walter. Another time, another life.

As Neville spoke, her attention wandered to the entrance, where Marshall McConner entered with a woman with cherry-red Cleopatra hair framing her pale face. Sonya, the manager from the White Lotus Spa.

"What's wrong?" Neville asked, glancing over his shoulder to follow Henny's gaze. "Oh, hey. That's Marshall." He waved.

Marshall waved back and smiled.

"You know him?" Henny asked.

"Yeah. Of course. We play golf together at the country club."

"How could you? Don't you—" She bit back the rest of the

yet, but I'm almost certain."

Neville frowned. "Are you sure? I've known Marshall—"

"I don't like him, and I don't think you should associate with him."

He stepped back. "Marshall is a golfing buddy of mine and—"

"Yeah, but you don't know him that well, do you? Because if you did, why don't you know he's dating that girl?"

"Well, that's true. Maybe I don't know him that well. What do you think he's done?"

She pressed her forehead. Something churned at the back of her brain, telling her to hush up now. She played it off.

"It happened several years ago. I remember reading about it in the paper, but I can't remember the details."

"You're making an awful big claim on very little evidence, Henny Wiley. You think he's involved in something bad enough that I should end my friendship with him?"

She nodded.

He reached out to stroke her cheek. "You're a dear woman. I tell you what, when you find out what Marshall did, you let me know. And if you still think he's too rotten to hang around, then I'll consider distancing myself from him."

Henny flushed and looked away. "I'm sorry. I don't have the right to tell you who to be friends with, and that's not what I'm trying to do."

"Oh, no, I get it. And I'm not exactly caving in." Neville chuckled. "I'm only saying I'll consider it. But you seem like a woman of strong character, so I think I can trust your judgment." Neville's hand dropped to massage her shoulder gently.

His hand seemed strangely hot. "I appreciate the compliment." She wanted to touch him . . . to place her hand in the center of his chest . . . to . . .

Walter stood beside Neville, glaring at him. Now she felt warmer for a different reason. She waited for Walter to do something drastic.

He glowed brightly, then took a swing at Neville.

Neville tucked his hands in his pockets. "Mighty chilly out here tonight, isn't it?"

Henny glanced at Walter. "Sure is."

Neville stepped closer, touching her waist. "A kiss might warm things up." He smelled fresh, clean, and . . . warm.

"It might. But . . . " She looked down at her tennis shoes.

"Is this about McConner? I offered to reconsider my friendship with him if you prove his criminal behavior, but Henny, I'm not in the habit of letting the women in my life choose my friends, no more than I let my friends choose my women."

Women? Did he date one woman at a time, or enjoy juggling them? Is he dating another woman now? She needed to know where she stood.

She stepped back. "I think I should go inside. Thank you again."

"I think I understand. This is about Walter, isn't it?"

Henny glanced at Walter again. She didn't want to talk about him, especially with Neville—and while Walter listened. She already felt unsettled about eating at The Old Mill so close to their forty-fifth anniversary.

"Not really, I—"

Walter threw himself at Neville again but fell through.

"Hey, I get it. I understand. You miss him."

Her stomach twisted in on itself like a nest of snakes. Henny really didn't feel well now. Walter flew around the house in a rage, creating a wind each time he passed the porch. She didn't want Neville talking about Walter or poking into her past relationship with her late husband. The heat moved from her body to concentrate in her face.

Henny jerked her house keys from her purse. "I need to go. Good night." She shoved the key in the door, and ducked inside before Neville could say anything more.

Walter sat on the couch, fuming. Big puffs of tobacco smoke rose from his grouchy image. "Hope you enjoyed yourself tonight," he sneered.

Henny flopped down in her recliner. She didn't have the energy for another fight. "I didn't. There. Does that make you happy? We went to The Old Mill, and I spent most of the dinner thinking about you and our upcoming anniversary, and how I am dreading it."

"I suppose that's *my* fault too?"

"Isn't it? In part, at least? I mean, when you're married to someone, you're responsible for your own happiness, and theirs. That's what it means to take care of each other."

"I did my best to make you happy!" he shouted. "Why do you think I worked so hard all the time? To buy you a house, clothes, a car. To provide for you."

Henny twisted around in her chair, kicking over a stack of plastic boxes and bags. "Do you think that's all I ever wanted? What about taking care of my *heart*? A bouquet occasionally. Taking me on vacation every now and then, without me having to run myself ragged, doing all the planning and organizing, while you sit by, like a lump on a log, offering no help, no opinions, nothing. How about planning a date night, and surprising me with it? You never did any of those things. And whenever I suggested something romantic, you called me crazy and demanding."

"What are you talking about? I worked my butt off every day. Whenever you needed errands run, I ran the errands. Whatever you asked me to do, I did it."

"And there's the problem. I got so tired of asking. Your idea of a romantic time involved sitting on the couch in our pajamas, and watching TV while we ate supper, night after night after stupid night. Neville planned two great nights out this week, which is more than you and I did in the entire last year of our marriage."

Walter said softly, "I may not have been some romantic fool like you see on the silly soap operas you watch. Maybe a little rough around the edges. Maybe even boring. But I'll tell you this, woman, I loved you. Love you still. And I promise you, throughout our entire marriage, whatever room you walked into, I felt love. Maybe I didn't give you the attention or romance you deserved, but I gave you everything in me, right until the very end. And then some."

He continued. "Anything I ever did, I did for you—your happiness, your protection, your security, and your provision. You. No, I didn't give you fancy flowers, and candies, and whirlwind dream vacations. My love grew out of clay and earth, of the practical stuff of life. For *you*. Always. You never worried about my whereabouts, or any other woman. And in the end, isn't that much more important than all the flowers, and vacations, and romance in the world?" He rose, his light growing dimmer. "I hope your new man can do all that. Good luck, Henny." He flashed into nothingness.

Henny wiped her eyes across the sleeve of his sweatshirt. When the tears didn't stop, she pulled a box of tissues from the side table, and cuddled them, while she watched *Gunsmoke*—one of Walter's favorite shows.

19

Henny dreamed strange, vague images involving Marshall McConner, Starla, Neville, and a dead Jenna Lawson wearing red glittery shoes and whistling *The Andy Griffith Show* theme. She blinked her eyes open, unable to recall any details.

She floated into the kitchen on the dreamy recollection of Neville wanting to kiss her. As she made her coffee and popped some frozen waffles into the toaster, she imagined his kiss.

The scent of burning snapped her from her thoughts. She scraped off the burned parts with a butter knife, microwaved some bacon, and poured a cup of coffee. Settling in her recliner, she flipped through the TV channels to the local news.

The reporter's blonde hair whipped around her face as she detailed the story. "The sheriff's office says the body of an unidentified partially clothed young woman, found this morning in a ditch off the Bluegrass Parkway South, came to the attention of two tourists whose car broke down nearby."

Henny's food went down her throat as though covered in thorns. She called Sheriff Basham, her fingers shaking.

He answered, the sound of cars swooshing by in the background.

"Sheriff, this is Henny Wiley. I'm sorry to bother you, but I saw the story about the girl y'all found. Is it Starla Elliott?"

"I'm afraid so."

"Oh, Lord . . . " Henny's voice broke. "That poor girl."

"More than that, I can't really tell you, Mrs. Wiley."

"Thank you, Sheriff. I appreciate it." Henny hung up without saying goodbye. She broke into breathless sobs.

Her head throbbed with a dull pain, and she abandoned her breakfast in favor of two Tylenol pills.

The neighbor's dog barked as if to wake the dead. Not unusual, but this time it sounded high and panicked. Urgent. She peeked out the window over the kitchen sink but saw nothing strange.

One of Jenna's flyers lay on top of her kitchen table, and she studied the sweet face smiling at her from the paper.

Walter came into sight beside her, singing an old Hank Williams song, "Hey, good lookin', whatcha got cookin'?" He looked sweet in his flannel robe, John Deere cap, and black socks.

"Morning."

"What's wrong?"

She explained everything to Walter, who thought for a moment, then said, "That's awful. I haven't seen the new girl come through, but as soon as I do, I can tell her you tried."

"Thanks." She knocked some papers off the kitchen chair and sat down. "Lot of good my efforts did."

"At least those girls knew somebody cared."

Henny nodded. "I guess."

"But you know what your biggest problem is?"

"What?"

"The killer is still out there." He pulled his pipe out of his robe pocket and puffed a few rings into the air. "Seems to me there's still something you can do."

Henny changed into her clothes from last night. She wanted to get to the library as soon as possible. The sweatshirt and jeans smelled a bit like the restaurant, so she sprayed herself with Febreze, and dashed out the door, planning to drive with the heater blasting, and the window down, to air out her clothes and hair.

When she reached her truck, she saw a note stuck to her windshield.

BACK OFF OR ELSE!

That explained Khan's barking this morning. The writing on the paper appeared scrawled with a black marker. She flipped the page over. A mint-green border filled with white palm fronds. Except on the top of the page—no border. The very top looked cut off. Why? Someone trying to hide a logo, or letterhead? Possibly, because this looked a great deal like personal stationery.

Rattled, Henny looked around the neighborhood. A light breeze agitated the trees, but the street appeared otherwise quiet. She jumped in the truck, locking her door. Henny watched her surroundings as she backed out of the driveway.

She relaxed a little as she moved further from the house. Henny glanced again at the note on the seat beside her. Her fingers clutched the steering wheel tighter until her knuckles turned white.

Not to be easily put off, especially by some coward hiding behind an anonymous note on her windshield, she headed toward downtown, hugging the circular road that wrapped around the courthouse. Halfway around, she whipped to the right, and followed Maple Street to the end, where the Plumridge Public Library sat nestled under a shield of yellow and red maple trees.

The library, a brown octagonal building with automatic doors that swept open, hit her with warm air. Halloween window clings of pumpkins and black cats stuck to the glass doors. Inside, paper bats hung from the ceiling, and Halloween books perched on display in front of the main circulation desk. Cartoonish cut-outs of ghosts, witches, jack-o'-lanterns, and various monsters sat scattered about.

The air smelled faintly of old books. As Henny approached the reference section, the librarian, a petite woman with long gold-red, frizzy hair and round glasses, popped up. Her rosebud lips parted. "Hi, Mrs. Wiley, how are you today?"

Henny nodded. "Hello yourself, Charlotte. I need to look up something about someone. Any chance you have time to help?"

The boredom drained from Charlotte's face. "Oh yes, yes. What do you need to know?"

"I want to find out who owns the White Lotus Spa. I have a sneaking suspicion it's Marshall McConner. I also want to see if he owns anything else."

"Okay. How old is the spa? Is it more than twenty years old?"

"No. I think it's only been around for about five years."

"Oh, good. We can probably find everything online." Charlotte sat down at the computer terminal and typed in her password.

Henny sat beside her. Charlotte's spider fingers flew over the keys.

"Here we go. The White Lotus. Says it's owned by Apex Properties, LLC."

"And who owns that?"

"Hm." Charlotte's eyes rolled upward to think for a moment. Then, she typed again. "According to this, the president of Apex Properties is Marshall McConner."

"Does it say what else this Apex owns?"

Charlotte hit a few keys and leaned her elbow on the desk, toying with her bottom lip as she scrolled through the screen. "Hm. A few apartment complexes. One in Louisville, one in Lexington, one in Elizabethtown. Let's see . . . " She scrolled further down. "A couple of small used car lots. One in Frankfort, one in Danville. And five restaurants. Two in Louisville, two in Lexington, and one in Richmond. This guy must be rolling in dough."

"What are the names of the restaurants in Louisville?"

Charlotte clicked on something. "One is the Rosy Raven Pub, and the other is . . . "

Anticipation and fear twined together within Henny. She might explode if Charlotte said . . .

"The Gilded Lily."

Henny gasped. "I heard about that place on the news the other night. It's the restaurant in Louisville where the FBI broke up that human labor ring."

"Oh, wow. That's wild. It's happening in so many places these days. And it's hard to find the victims because they move them around from place to place constantly." Charlotte placed a cold hand on Henny's. "Are you okay?"

"I'm fine, thank you. Does it say who else owns Apex Properties?"

Charlotte clicked around for what seemed an hour. "Mm. I don't see anyone else listed. Maybe they're silent partners? The only thing I'm seeing is Marshall McConner listed as founder and president."

Henny stood. "Thank you, dear, for helping me. You always were my favorite student. Please tell your momma I say hello."

Henny practically ran to her truck, dialing Sheriff Basham's number. She unlocked the door and climbed in. When his voicemail picked up, she left a hurried message. "Hey, Sheriff, Henny Wiley here. I just left the library, where I discovered Marshall McConner is founder and president of Apex Properties. That group owns the Gilded Lily *and* the White Lotus. I'm telling you, that man's a trafficker, and I bet he's responsible for both Jenna and Starla's deaths. But maybe you already discovered all that yourself."

Henny ended the call and stared out over the steering wheel, watching a squirrel skip up a tree trunk. "There must be something more I can do. But what?"

A horn sounded behind her, causing her to jump.

She started her truck, pulled out of the library parking lot, and turned right.

GRAY SKIES LOOMED over the Tanbark apartment complex where Bruce's yellow car gleamed like a beacon. Henny climbed the stairs and walked down the breezeway to Bruce and Prue's apartment. She knocked on the door.

Bruce called from within, "Hold on."

The door opened. Upon seeing her, he rolled his eyes and said, "You again? Lady, if you don't leave me alone, I'm going to call the sheriff."

"Go ahead. I'm working with them." Okay, technically a lie, but it sounded good, and might lend some authority, and credibility, to her presence, and maybe induce him to talk to her. The wind blew fiercely, and the temperature seemed to drop by the second.

"Five minutes. Then I never want to see you again." Bruce stepped aside and opened the door wider. "The only reason I'm doing this is because my grandma told me to respect my elders."

"I hate to see what disrespect looks like," Henny said. She did not want to go inside the home of a potential murder suspect. "If you don't mind, let's talk outside."

He stepped out in bare feet, his toes peeking out from under the hem of his holey jeans. A loose Metallica T-shirt draped over his lean body. "What do you want now? I told you, and the sheriff, I didn't do nothing."

Henny squinted. "That's a double negative. So, you *did* do something?"

"Huh? I did nothing to Jenna."

"Other than stalking her?" The wind released a lonesome howl.

He pulled a pack of cigarettes out of his front pocket. He drew one out and lit it, shielding the flame from the wind. Bruce drew deep and blew the smoke to the side. "You're crazy. Like I said, I never hurt her."

"All I want to know is if you followed her the day she disappeared. Or if you saw where she went. Anything at all?"

Bruce huffed. "Lady, I don't know what you want from me. I already answered all these questions."

Henny leaned toward him. "What about your girlfriend?"

Bruce glared at her with disgust. "Exactly what are you saying?"

"I'm saying your girlfriend is unbalanced, and violently jealous, and she's just the sort of person to hurt Jenna, or any other woman who might get in her way."

Confusion twisted his features. Henny pulled the note from her purse and showed him.

"Did you, or your girlfriend, leave this on my car?"

"What?" He drew from his cigarette and turned for the door. "We're done here."

She shook it in the air. "Did you leave this?"

"No. Don't be ridiculous. I don't even think about you until you show up to harass me. Get out of here. Now."

"Do you know Starla Elliott?"

"Look, lady, I need you to understand something. If you come back here, you won't leave. Got it?" He stepped inside his apartment and slammed the door.

Henny growled to herself, marched back to her truck, and drove straight to the sheriff's office to turn the note in as evidence.

She met Marshall McConner as he exited the sheriff's department. Dark circles ringed his eyes. He paused to speak with her.

"Henny Wiley. You are quite a thorn in my side."

"Good. I hope so. A man like you shouldn't rest easy at night."

"What are you talking about?"

"The Gilded Lily."

He frowned and glanced around. "What about it?"

"Don't play dumb. Everyone knows about the human trafficking moving through there."

"That's untrue. It's a misunderstanding."

"Ha!" She pointed her finger at him. "I'll tell you something else, mister. I know you're doing the same thing at the White Lotus, and I'm going to prove it. When I'm done, you're going to sit in prison, where you belong, for the rest of your life."

Marshall chuckled and walked away without another word.

Henny entered the building and slammed the note down on Rosita's desk. Though the sheriff took her statement, he lacked the confidence that anything could be done about the situation.

"Well, can't you send it to a lab and get DNA, or something?"

"Ma'am, with all due respect, this isn't TV, and there's probably not much we can retrieve since you handled it already."

"Can you do nothing at all?"

"Like what, Mrs. Wiley?"

"I don't know. A stakeout or something. Khan's more useful than you are, at this point."

He scratched his head. "Ma'am, I don't know who Khan is, and I want to help you, I really do, but this is nothing more than a note. Anything broken, or stolen?"

"No."

"Then in all likelihood, it's probably just some kids messing with you. I mean, it's Halloween season—"

"And what if it's not? What if this is serious? Are y'all going to stand by and let someone hurt me?"

"No, of course not. But we also have laws to follow, and we need more evidence than a note. *And* we have incredibly limited resources."

"I see. So, you're not going to help a tax-paying citizen in this town? Is that what you're telling me?"

"I'm sorry that's what you're hearing. My recommendation, Mrs. Wiley, is to have someone stay with you, if you feel you need additional protection. My other recommendation is to get a camera put on your house to catch the person, or persons, attempting to harass you. They're fairly cheap on Amazon, and pretty easy to set up. And if you're able to catch the person, or persons, in the act, then I can do something."

"So basically, you're telling me to do your job for you?"

The sheriff tucked his thumbs in his belt. "No, ma'am. I'm not saying that at all. I'm saying we need help sometimes. That we can't be everywhere at once. I have a small force running a county of fifty thousand people. That's a lot of people to serve and protect, for a staff of twenty people. And even though Franklin County is small compared to others, and is relatively peaceful, there's more than enough going on to keep them hopping."

The anger rising in her suddenly deflated. "Sounds like y'all are outnumbered."

He shrugged. "Technically, we are. So, what I'm saying is, to make a case stick, I need hard, undeniable evidence."

"Alright, Sheriff. I won't take up any more of your time then. Good day."

"Good day, Mrs. Wiley. We'll keep the note here in our evidence room, just in case."

Henny headed back to her truck. She didn't know anything about shopping online. She preferred shopping in person so she could touch, see, and feel the things she wanted to buy. After all, that's what made her treasures special.

Henny watched cars and people go by. She called Ida Mae. "Do you know anything about buying from an Amazon?"

"What on earth are you talking about? Have you been in the Happy Pappy bourbon again?"

"Lord, no. I haven't touched that stuff since last Christmas when I nearly vomited up my own shoes. I'm never touching it again."

"You can't blame the bourbon because you're a lightweight. I told you to go easy on that Christmas punch."

"Are you going to tell me about the Amazon, or not?"

Ida Mae laughed. "Of course. Come over to my house, and I'll show you."

20

Henny arrived home several hours later with a bag full of Hop-pin' Jalapeno's tacos for supper.

"Walter?"

He didn't answer.

Henny set down her purse and keys on top of a box in the kitch-en. She moved toward the living room to settle into her recliner with her supper, but stopped short when her cell phone rang.

"Hello?"

"Hey there, sweet lady."

Neville.

"Hi. How are you?" Awkwardness and tension knotted her shoul-der blades. She didn't know for sure if she wanted to continue with Neville. After all, didn't birds of a feather flock together? How often did good people knowingly befriend and congregate with criminals?

"I want to apologize for last night. I hope I didn't upset you too much."

"That's okay. Maybe I overreacted a little too."

He chuckled. "Nah. Don't worry about it. So, I called because I'm hoping to make it up to you. We can go dancing if you like."

Henny wanted to dance. But she didn't want to dance. She leaned against the refrigerator.

Glancing around the kitchen, she saw, as if for the first time, the piles of boxes, bags, newspapers, magazines, and empty containers. The thin paths leading from the sink to the stove, to the pantry, to the fridge, to the living room allowed her to remember what the floor looked like—an old gold linoleum, with dark brown concentric squares in the center.

Where did all this stuff come from? When did it get here? Her vision tilted as though looking in a funhouse mirror. Her head felt stuffed full of cotton, and her thoughts seemed dim and hazy, like lights shining through a thick fog.

"Hello? Henny? Are you there?"

"Yes. I'm here." Her voice sounded far away. Nausea gripped her throat.

"Do you want to go out tonight?"

"I'm not feeling too well at the moment."

"Oh," he said flatly. "I see. You're still upset with me."

Heaviness weighed in her limbs. "No. I'm not. Really. I'm, uh—"

"Are you sure? You're not upset?"

"I'm sure."

He paused. "Okay. Can I call you another time to ask you out?"

"Sure."

His voice lifted. "Good. Maybe then you won't be sick."

"I hope not."

Henny hung up the phone and picked her way through the piles in the hallway to the bedroom she once shared with Walter. Boxes, bags, clothes, shoes, belts, books, and hats loaded down the bed. Henny wanted to lie down. Since Walter died, she slept on the couch, or the recliner. Maybe she should clear the bed so she could sleep properly. But as she considered where to begin with cleanup, where to store the stuff, her vision adjusted to the pile on the bed in the same way one might adjust to a foul smell. Maybe another day then. She felt tired and heavy.

Henny left the room to stretch out on the living room recliner, with her bag of tacos, and the nightly news, followed by *Jeopardy!*

IN THE WEE hours of the morning, Henny heard a crash of glass, quickly followed by a thud, a gunning engine, and squealing tires—and Khan, barking like an idiot. She jolted up in the recliner and stared at the television. A blast of cold air hit her in the face, and the curtain in the window beside her billowed.

The haze of sleep lifted, allowing her to slowly piece together the event. Chunks of glass covered the piles of bags in front of the TV stand. A few feet away, a rock covered with paper, and held in place with duct tape, lay nested on top of a shopping bag full of Lydia's baby clothes. Henny reached for it, then, recalling her meeting with the sheriff earlier, pulled back her hand. She grabbed her cell phone and called Sheriff Basham.

21

Within fifteen minutes, Sheriff Basham and a deputy unknown to her stood in Henny's living room, looking around as if something might jump out and attack them.

"So, uh . . . " The sheriff took in the room. "I don't mean to be rude, but you live in this?"

"Yes. So?"

"With all due respect, Mrs. Wiley, this is a health hazard."

"I didn't call you here for comments on my decor. I called you because of this." She pointed at the broken window.

The sheriff picked his way through the piles, nearly losing his balance.

A deputy took pictures of the window, the broken glass, and the rock. The sheriff put on his latex gloves and opened the paper, revealing a mint-green border filled with white palm fronds, the same as Henny found before on her car. In large red words, it said *You're next.*

"See," Henny said. "I'm being threatened. You have to do something."

"You're right. Let's start at the beginning." The sheriff took note of her statement. He glanced around. "Did you order a camera like I recommended?"

"I have, but it'll take a few days to ship."

"Good. In the meantime, I highly encourage you to clean up your home, so I don't have to report you." A pleading tone edged his voice. "I don't want to call adult services on you, so I'll give you a month."

"This situation"—she motioned around the room——"doesn't concern you."

"I'm afraid it does, ma'am. This here is a health and safety issue. If something caught fire, everything else goes up like a match. Or, if God forbid, you have a health issue, how are the EMTs supposed to reach you? Do you understand?"

The fog descended on her mind again. "Yep. Sure do. I'll try."

"I can give you the names of people who specialize—"

Henny opened the front door. "No, no, no. That's fine. I can do it myself." As the sheriff stepped out, she said, "What happens if I don't clean up?"

"You might lose all your stuff, and your house, or even be placed in a home."

"You mean a nursing home?"

"More like assisted living, but yes."

She grew rigid, the screeching crickets filling her ears.

"Good night, Mrs. Wiley. If you need anything—"

She shut the door and locked it.

An icy wind blasted through the hole in the window. She hugged herself and shivered, gazing stupidly at the room. Clean up the house or lose the home she and Walter bought together soon after they wed. Leaving Walter behind seemed unacceptable.

Henny picked up an empty shopping bag. Maybe just throw this one thing away. Fear electrified her, and she clutched the handles. Her palms grew sweaty. No, she might use this bag again. She might need to carry something in it. Panic fluttered in her chest.

No, not the bag then, so what about this empty cola bottle? Henny picked it off the table. Maybe this?

"What are you doing?" Walter asked.

She gazed at him. He seemed unfamiliar to her. It felt like ages since he visited her last. She didn't respond.

"What's wrong with this window? You need to patch it up, so the heat doesn't kick on. It costs too much to heat this house."

Henny looked at the shoebox at her feet. Boxes are always the best things to save. Lots of things can be stored in boxes.

"Yoo-hoo!" Walter waved his hand in front of her face. "The hole. The window. What's the matter with you?"

"He said I might lose the house."

"What? Why? Who said that?"

"The sheriff. He said if I don't clean up this mess, I might lose the house. He said he's going to check back soon, and if the place isn't cleaned up, he's going to report me."

Walter puffed up and glowed bright. "You'll lose this house over my dead body."

IDA MAE ARRIVED early the next morning. "I got breakfast," she sang. "Raspberry lemon scones. Coffee brewing yet?"

"Help yourself," Henny called from the living room. She never fell back to sleep after the sheriff left. Instead, she taped cardboard and plastic over the hole in her window, and brushed the glass into a jar so she could keep the shards. After, she made coffee and sat zombie-like in the recliner, staring at the television infomercials, waiting for the news to come on.

Ida Mae entered the living room with a mug and the box of scones. "What the devil happened here?"

Henny looked at her.

"Henny? What happened, hon?"

Henny told her everything as Ida Mae eased down on the end of the sofa and made a place for the scones and coffee. "I guess they think I'm some mousy old lady who will shrivel up and die from fear, but these idiots don't realize who they're dealing with." She shoved her sweatshirt sleeves up to her elbows.

"Have you told the sheriff's department?"

"Of course. The sheriff himself came out here early this morning. But he sure managed to get on my poop list awfully fast."

"What do you mean?"

Henny informed her sister of what Sheriff Basham said about taking away her home and dumping her in assisted living.

"He's threatening to take my treasures. He can't just come into my home and dictate how I live. Who does he think he is?" Henny sobbed. "Oh, what am I going to do, Ida Mae? Walter says they'll take my house over his dead body, but—"

"Walter? Honey, are you trying to tell me he spoke to you?"

Henny froze. "I, uh . . . I guess I dreamed that part. I'm all worked up." She grabbed a newspaper from the side table and fanned herself, touching her hot cheeks. "I need to calm down. Sorry. The sheriff just really upset me."

Pity warmed Ida Mae's eyes. "Hon, you know I love you. You're my sister, and my best friend. Because I love you, I want the best for you. And I have to say, I'm with the sheriff on this one."

"You can't mean that. You want to separate me from my treasures too?"

"Henny, this stuff isn't treasure. Most of it is garbage."

Henny lurched forward. "How dare you—"

"Hold on. I'm not going to let anyone take your house away. We'll talk about this later once you calm down a little. Our first priority is breakfast." Ida Mae handed Henny a scone. "Okay?"

Henny nodded.

"Now, eat."

They nibbled breakfast and watched the news. The anchorwoman opened with the story about the Gilded Lily.

"Oh, did you hear about that?" Ida Mae said.

"I did. It's awful. Those poor people. Let's listen."

The anchorwoman said, "The FBI, in cooperation with local agencies, arrested three alleged ringleaders of the labor trafficking ring busted at the Gilded Lily in Louisville. A suspicious employee at the Pink Flamingo, a motel on the border of Jefferson and Franklin County, made the call. Sarah Gonzalez joins us live with more details."

A reporter appeared on the screen. "Thank you, Amber. We are here with Sheriff Basham, and Grayson Beale, manager of the Pink

Flamingo. Mr. Beale, what made you suspicious enough to make the call?"

An older man with thinning gray hair and thick glasses spoke. "Three girls, with lotus flower tattoos on their inner arms, came in with a big burly guy, and another guy. They seemed scared. One of the girls asked to use the restroom in the lobby, and the big guy stood by the door, which I thought odd. When she came out, she said the toilet broke. I went in to inspect it and saw 'help me' written in lipstick on the wall. So, I called the sheriff." He shrugged. "There's a lot of this in hospitality, so we're taught to spot it. But I am shocked it happened here. We aren't fancy, but we try to run a clean establishment. I'm just happy I could help."

"And I'm sure those women are happy too, knowing they're safe now. Thank you." The reporter spoke to the sheriff. "Sheriff Basham, are you seeing much of this activity in Kentucky?"

"I am. You might be surprised how many businesses are using forced labor."

"Are you working on ferreting out other rings in the area?"

"Yes. I can't go into too many details, but we're currently working with the FBI in tracking down the other businesses that are part of this ring. We think it runs between Ohio and Florida. Unfortunately, it's so large, and spread out, they can alert each other pretty quickly, and move the workers, or shut down, before we get to them."

"What are the signs of human trafficking? And what can someone do if they suspect such activity in their area?"

"A few simple things to look for are the same tattoo on multiple people, because sometimes traffickers brand their workers. Someone who seems very secretive, or fearful, especially in revealing details of their lives. Someone who seems to have limited freedom of movement. But the important thing to remember is trafficking can be difficult to detect because they move the workers around often to avoid detection. I encourage everyone to go to the Franklin County Sheriff's website. We have resources there to educate you on what to do if you suspect human trafficking."

Ida Mae shook her head. "Mm-mm. What is this world coming to?"

Henny stared at the large neon flamingo motel sign behind the reporter. Flamingoes. Florida. Palm trees. Palm trees. The stationery! She jumped up. "Ida Mae, we're going for a ride."

"Don't you want to at least change out of your pajamas?"

Henny glanced down at her red plaid pants and gray T-shirt with a sweet black kitten on the front claiming, I do what I want. "No time for that. Let's go." She grabbed her keys, threw a jacket over her outfit, and slid her feet into her gardening boots by the door.

Ida Mae followed. "At least pat down your crazy hair. It's sticking out all over the place."

Henny mashed down her hair as she marched across the frosty grass. Khan barked.

"What's going on? Why are you in such a hurry?" Ida Mae ran around the front of the truck and got in on the passenger side as Henny started the engine.

Henny blasted the heat and directed the vents to her feet. She threw the truck into gear and backed out. "I'm going out to the Pink Flamingo to see if the paper from the notes I received came from there. If I can make the connection, it might help the sheriff."

THE AUTOMATIC DOORS swooshed open at the Pink Flamingo.

Grayson Beale smiled from behind the front desk. "May I help you ladies?"

Henny leaned on the counter. "I have a strange question, but can I please see the stationery you place in the rooms here?"

Grayson examined her quizzically. "Uh, sure. Let me see if I can find . . . " He rummaged through a drawer. "You mean this?" He placed a notepad on the counter and slid it across.

Henny gasped and showed it to Ida Mae. "That's it. That's the paper."

She turned to Grayson. "Can I have a sheet of this? I'm happy to pay you for it, if necessary."

"No, of course you can have it." He tore off a piece and gave it to her.

"Thank you so much. C'mon." Henny tapped her sister's arm. "Let's take this out to the sheriff."

SHERIFF BASHAM RESPONDED to Henny's presence curtly. He didn't invite her back to his office this time but met her in the lobby. He assumed a power stance. "Mrs. Wiley. How can I help you?"

She handed him the paper. "I got this at the Pink Flamingo Motel. Look familiar?"

He studied it. "Sure does. Now, that's interesting."

"Right? Don't you think the person who's leaving notes at my house is somehow connected to the trafficking ring?"

"Possibly."

"I think it's Marshall McConner. Maybe he is trying to intimidate or silence me."

"Good luck with that," chuckled Ida Mae.

Henny glared at her. "This is serious."

Ida Mae pulled an invisible zipper across her lips.

"We interviewed McConner a few times already, but there is no connection between him and the Pink Flamingo yet."

"But he owns the Gilded Lily. Isn't that enough to arrest him?"

"Without going into details on an active case, it's not that simple. There are other things we're looking at with him. We're hoping he'll give us a list of other people involved, bigger people than him. There are a lot of moving parts to this."

"That's not good enough."

"Henny!" Ida Mae warned.

The sheriff's jaw knotted. He spoke through clenched teeth. "It will have to be good enough. There are things going on I'm not at liberty to divulge to a civilian. Mrs. Wiley, go home, clean up your house, and stop playing detective. It will not go well if you continue down the path you're on. I can promise you that."

22

Henny marched out the door, with Ida Mae hard on her heels.
"Are you trying to get yourself arrested, Henny? I can't believe you talked to a sheriff of the law that way. Mama and Daddy can't be happy with you right now."

Henny spun around. "Well, then it's a good thing they're not here to see it. I'm tired of this nonsense. What am I supposed to do? Just lay down and take it? No, ma'am. Absolutely not. Plumridge is a good place, full of good people, and I don't like what's going on right now. I don't want these big city problems in this tiny town, threatening our way of life. I don't want us to worry all the time about our safety. So, I'm going to do something about it."

"And just what do you think you're going to do, Nancy Drew? All you're going to do is get in the way of the officers and their investigation and get yourself in some deep trouble. That's what."

"No, I won't get in trouble, but I'm going to do everything I can to help the sheriff get this mess out of our town, once and for all." She opened the truck, and they climbed in. Henny glared at her sister. "Are you in, or out?"

Ida Mae scowled out the window, contemplating. "I guess I'm going with you. If nothing else, to make sure you don't get yourself killed."

Henny parked behind the strip mall housing the Ladybug's Consignment shop, the White Lotus, and Sassy Styles. She opened her door to get out.

Ida Mae grabbed her arm. "What do you think you're doing?"

"I'm going to dig in these dumpsters to see if I can find anything else."

"Don't you think forensics did that already?"

"Are you coming, or not?"

"Fine," Ida Mae growled, and slid out of the truck.

"I want to start here at Ladybug's. Keep a lookout."

Henny removed her diving kit, quickly completed her set up, and stood on the stepladder. "Get me a long, sturdy stick." Her voice echoed from inside the bin. "There might be something in my truck."

A few moments later, Ida Mae shoved a broken broom handle at her, along with the directive to hurry up.

Henny poked and stirred through the contents of the dumpster. A cute stuffed giraffe caught her eye, even though it needed fixing up. She hooked the stick under the neck ribbon and lifted it out of the dumpster. Henny handed it to Ida Mae. "Hold on to this."

"Are you kidding me? You're supposed to be looking for evidence, and you're out here collecting junk?"

Henny lifted her head out of the bin. "Hush. I can multitask, dang it."

"I don't have all day. I'm due at Eileen Cartwright' house to work on a quilt for the Expo in Lexington in March."

"Fine." Henny climbed out and dragged her kit over to the dumpster behind the White Lotus. "God forbid I keep you from your fancy quilting for your fancy Expo," she sneered, wiggling her torso with sarcasm.

"You're just lucky I'm out here helping you at all, you old grouchy heifer."

"With a sister like you, who needs enemies?" Henny jammed the stick inside, and poked around.

Ida Mae leaned against the dumpster. "I know you don't mean that."

Henny poked and shifted the garbage once more. "Hey, what's that?" She stretched further into the bin. "Is that what I think it is?" Henny worked the stick back and forth and stepped off the step-ladder.

A glittery red shoe dangled from the end of the broom handle.

Henny held it up. "This is Jenna's. I have its mate at home."

Ida Mae gasped. "You have evidence in an active investigation at your house? Did you lose your ever-loving mind? You're going to be in so much trouble."

"Oh, hush. I am not." Jenna's shoe, so pretty and glittery. Henny tucked it into her sparkly pink collection bag.

The back door to the spa slammed open, and a girl with frizzy, bleach-blonde hair marched out. Her anorectic frame lurched toward the dumpster. She stopped short when she noticed Henny and Ida Mae.

Henny held out her hand as if to still a scared feral cat. The girl's high cheekbones and bony limbs did give her a feline quality.

"It's okay. Are you here against your will, sweetie?"

The girl took a step back.

"Are you being hurt? I want to help you. My truck is right there. Come with us."

The girl glanced over her skeletal shoulder and turned her wide feline gaze back to Henny.

"C'mon, hon." Henny beckoned the girl to follow her.

She whispered, "I can't."

The door cracked open, and a voice called, "Angel?"

Henny and Ida Mae ducked behind the dumpster, and pressed fingers to their mouths, sending a silent signal to Angel to not reveal their presence. Henny peeked around the corner as a woman passed through the door. Sonya. She looked almost unrecognizable in her casual clothes and no-makeup face.

"Angel, what's taking so long? Your appointment is here."

"Sorry. I'm coming."

"Hurry up. Time is money."

Angel loped toward the dumpster and tossed a box inside. She flashed an anguished glance at Henny and returned to the building. Sonya looked around suspiciously, shoved Angel over the threshold, and closed the door.

"Let's get out of here." Ida Mae dashed from the hiding spot, with Henny close behind.

As they passed the alley between Ladybug's and the White Lotus, a dark sedan shot out, nearly hitting them before it slammed on its brakes. Marshall McConner. Henny started to dart around the front of the vehicle, but McConner pushed the car forward, effectively cutting her and Ida Mae off from their truck.

The beefy guy, Rob, rolled down his window to reveal the barrel of a pistol.

"Oh crap, he's got a gun!" Ida Mae shrieked, as Henny shouted, "Run!"

They spun and headed the other direction toward the back door of Sassy's.

"Hey!" Rob shouted. He got out of the car and charged them. "Come back here."

Henny passed Ida Mae and grabbed her arm. Her breath came in great gasps. They reached the door and tried to open it. Locked. They beat on the door and shouted, glancing over their shoulders at the beast of a man lunging toward them.

The knob jiggled. Henny grabbed it, and jerked it back, almost throwing Dottie to the ground with the force of her pull. Henny and Ida Mae rushed in, locking the door behind them.

Ida Mae shouted, "They're trying to kill us!"

Henny dashed toward the front door and locked it. As she lowered the blinds, Ida Mae and Dottie, came from the back room.

"I'm calling 9-1-1 this minute." Dottie picked up the phone, while Henny and Ida Mae peeked through the blinds.

Dottie's voice shook. "I have two ladies here. They say a man is trying to kill them."

Henny shouted, "It's Marshall McConner, and his henchman, Rob."

Dottie hung up the phone. "They're sending someone now."

"Oh crap! There he is." Henny backed away from the window. She looked around for a weapon, and, unable to find anything satisfactory, grabbed a pair of scissors. Henny stood en garde, ready to lunge if the men came through the door.

Ida Mae ducked behind the counter. "Y'all hide. Henny, don't stand there in the open like a fool."

Henny and Dottie joined Ida Mae behind the counter. Dottie reached into her purse and pulled out a pink pistol.

Henny's brows shot up. "You're packing?"

"Yes ma'am. I told you I got me a gun when those men started hanging out around here. I ain't afraid to use it neither."

The phone rang, and the three women jumped. Henny answered.

"This isn't over, Henny Wiley. You're officially on my list." Henny recognized the voice as Marshall McConner.

"Well, I have a list of my own, mister. And the sheriff on my side."

The sound of breaking glass filled the salon, and the women screamed. Henny peeked over the edge of the counter to see Rob's beefy hand reaching in to unlock the door.

"Run!" Henny shouted. She and Ida Mae pushed themselves to their feet.

"Get in the storeroom," Dottie whispered, shoving them toward the back. "I'll cover you."

Henny hemmed. "Wait—"

Sirens sounded in the distance.

Dottie shouted at her, "Go now!"

The men burst in as Dottie popped up like a trained soldier and fired off a couple of warning shots that zipped past the men, landing in the wall. Henny and Ida Mae ducked into the storeroom.

Henny didn't want to shut the door on Dottie, and her chance for acquiring safety. So, she poked her head out instead. "Dottie, get in here!"

Dottie skipped backward with her gun still drawn. Rob lifted his and came toward her. Henny jumped out and grabbed Dottie, pulling her into the room, and slamming the door behind them as Rob fired. The women pushed into a far corner behind a shelf. The sound of cracking wood filled the air.

Panic and dread choked off Henny's ability to breathe. She clutched Ida Mae's hand.

Another cracking sound, and the door popped open.

The women screamed. Dottie stepped out, poised to shoot.

Rob lifted his gun. "I got ya now."

A chorus of voices shouted, "Freeze! Hands in the air!" and Deputy Billy Sykes stepped up behind Rob. "Drop the gun. Push it back toward me. Get on your knees."

The large man followed the directives. Billy clapped cuffs on the man who could barely put his muscled arms behind his back, and Deputy Leticia Peele stepped up to get the prisoner to his feet.

Billy led Rob away, as Leticia marched into the storeroom. "You ladies can come out now. Everyone okay?"

Henny exhaled. "Yes. We're okay. Thank y'all for getting here so fast." She fell back against the wall.

ROB AND MARSHALL marched out to the parking lot, where a law enforcement van awaited them. Marshall snarled at her.

"I hope you're happy, you obnoxious crone." He lunged at her. Deputy Leticia caught his elbow and pulled him back in line. Marshall shouted, "I'll make you pay!"

"Hush up," Leticia hissed. "You're not going to do a thing, except threaten your way into more charges."

Ida Mae sidled up to Henny, and they hugged. "Thank heavens that's over, and we can all get back to normal."

Henny chuckled. Whatever normal is. After all, she lived with the ghost of her dead husband. "Let's go home," she said. She needed to see Walter.

23

Neville sat on Henny's porch.

Discomfort settled over her, as she parked her truck. She took a deep breath to gather a spark of energy and approached.

"Hey there, lovely lady." Neville rose from the porch swing to greet her.

Henny paused. "I don't mean to be rude, but what are you doing here?" Her socks felt like lead as she dragged toward him.

"Wanted to swing by and see you for a bit. Are you okay?"

Henny studied him. She stepped up on the porch.

"I have some bad news for you."

"Oh?"

"Marshall McConner got himself arrested today for his involvement in that human trafficking ring," she said. "And for trying to kill me, and two other women. And he may be responsible for the murders of Jenna Lawson and Starla Elliott, but that remains to be seen."

Neville stepped toward her and put his hands on her shoulders. "Are you okay?" he repeated.

"I'm fine. Now." Henny smoothed her hair. A piece of glass fell into her hand.

He wrapped an arm around her and hugged her. His body smelled fresh and woodsy. The tension drained from her shoulders.

"How terrifying for you."

"Yes, I'm just glad that creep is behind bars now."

Neville pulled away. "I guess I didn't know him as well as I thought."

Henny narrowed her eyes and locked them with his, as if to suck information out of him, but she saw only genuineness and honesty.

"Forced labor? Murder? That's—that's—"

"Evil."

Neville nodded. "I'm sorry you went through that. And I'm sorry I ever trusted him. Even for a minute. I hope you don't hold my bad judgment against me."

Henny searched his face. She couldn't really blame Neville for something his idiot friend did. "No. I guess not."

"He's lucky he's in jail. If I ever get my hands on him..."

"Everything's okay now. I'm just glad they broke up the ring before he hurt anyone else."

Neville rubbed her upper arm. "Well, the reason I'm here...I'm hoping you might go to dinner with me. That is, if you're not too beat up after your wild afternoon."

Henny leaned against the porch post and looked down at her shoes. "I don't know. I'm sorry if I'm being weird, but I'm going to shoot you straight. I'm concerned about your past. And maybe your present. I hear you enjoy being around the ladies a little too much."

He lifted his chin. "Ah. I see. Rumors."

Henny shrugged one shoulder. "I suppose so. I don't intend to be one in a long list of women." Her face grew hot. "I want to be the only one."

Neville's dark brows shot up. "I understand; however, we aren't exclusive yet. I'm not even sure you like me enough."

Walter emerged on the porch, leaning against a column. "So, do you like him? You do, don't you? You're going to run off with him. You'll forget all about me."

"That's not true," she said to Walter, while looking at Neville from the corner of her eye.

"So, you do like me?" Neville asked.

Henny needed to think quickly. She needed a chance. A chance for normality. A chance for companionship, and to no longer be lonely. Terribly lonely. Hatefully, painfully lonely. Henny deserved a chance for a life. And, above all, another chance for love.

"Henny?" Neville craned his neck to try to meet her eyes.

"Oh, uh, sorry."

"I get it." He started down the stairs.

Henny shot up. "Wait. No. I-I-I'm just struggling. It's been a while since . . . " She glanced at Walter, who fumed silently, glowing brighter and brighter. "Since my husband died. I guess I don't know how to behave anymore."

"We'll take things slow. I don't want to pressure you."

"Okay." Slow sounded good. "But what about the other ladies?"

"There are no other ladies."

"Oh." She flushed. "Okay."

"Then you'll give me a chance? Because I sure do want a chance with you."

"Okay. Me too."

Walter vanished into a pinpoint of light without a word, obviously not happy.

"Good." Neville reached out his hand, and Henny placed hers in his, feeling little calluses where he held the golf clubs. He placed a kiss on her middle knuckle.

Henny's heart leapt like a rabbit in her chest.

"Now . . . " He entwined his fingers in hers. "Let's go eat. I'm starving."

Henny's stomach growled in agreement. "Okay. Somewhere casual is best if that's okay. But I need to freshen up first."

He shrugged. "Okay, I don't mind waiting." He started for her house door.

"No!" she shouted, much louder than intended.

Neville jerked back as if burned by the doorknob. Puzzlement drifted over his features. "Um, I'm sorry?"

"I'm sorry. I can't let you inside."

"Why?"

"My house is a disaster." Not a lie. Her mind grappled for a feasible excuse. "Most people do spring cleaning, but I do fall cleaning. Always have. It's a tradition started by my great-grandma. And I'm moving furniture and—"

"I don't mind." He started for the door again.

Henny jumped in front of him, the doorknob jamming into her back. "But I do." She put her hand to the center of his chest. "It's too embarrassing. My momma might roll over in her grave if she knew I let a visitor into a messy house. I'll only be a minute."

"Okay, then," he said, irritation edging his voice. "I'll wait out here."

"Thank you. I'm sorry." She ducked into the house and locked the door. She pushed her way past boxes and bags to the bathroom, leaving a trail of clothes and shoes. She jumped in the shower, hoping Walter didn't try to delay her bathing proceedings. He didn't, and within twenty minutes, she stood on the porch, breathless, and ready to go.

"Thank you for waiting for me," she said. "Where do we want to eat?"

"How about the Old Kentucky Kitchen?"

Images of blueberry pancakes, crispy bacon, turnip greens, and country ham danced across her mind. "Yes. That's a great choice!"

Neville walked Henny around to the passenger side of his car.

Walter buzzed by them, fluttering their hair.

Neville looked around. "Hm. The wind is picking up." He opened the door for her. "My lady."

Henny ducked inside. He closed the door and jogged around the front, while she buckled herself in the seat.

After starting the engine and buckling his seatbelt, Neville pushed buttons and turned knobs on the dashboard. He popped a CD into the player. "I got this the other day. I really like it. It's *Country Music's Greatest Hits from the 70s and 80s*. George Jones, Merle Haggard, Kenny Rogers, Dolly Parton, Hank Williams Jr. All the greats."

"Oh, sounds fun."

"Family Tradition" came on, filling the car with honky-tonk rhythms laced with the dancing high notes of a fiddle. They sang along, smiling, as Henny bopped her head, and Neville drummed the steering wheel.

Neville turned right, driving toward the outskirts of Plumridge, where the Old Kentucky Kitchen, called The Kitchen by locals, sat among other restaurants, and hotels, near the connections to Interstates 75 and 64. The Kitchen came complete with a nifty little gift shop flush with trinkets, toys, décor, cookware, and other treasures.

In the middle of the lyric, "Why must you live out the songs that you wrote . . . " Henny sneezed. And sneezed. And sneezed. She sniffled. "Excuse me."

"Bless you." Neville glanced at her, then back at the road, turning left.

She rummaged through her handbag. "I don't have a single tissue in here."

"Check the glove box."

Henny opened the compartment. A pile of cords, restaurant napkins and straws, a broken ice scraper, and a few papers spilled out onto the floor. "Oh shoot." Holding a napkin to her nose, she leaned over, picked up the items, shoved them back into the compartment, and slammed the door shut.

Neville pulled into The Kitchen's parking lot. "Whew! Packed house tonight," he said. He circled the lot twice before catching a van pulling out of its spot. "Lucky break. Didn't want to end up at Taco Bell." He chuckled, and they exited the car.

As Henny got out, she noticed her untied shoe. "Hold on." She knelt down, only then noticing a fallen paper from the glove box, now lodged under the seat.

She pulled it out, planning to return it to its rightful spot, when she noticed a Miami, Florida, address scrawled in thick ink across the blank side. The "M" consisted of a strange block formation, like the writer drew three vertical lines, and capped it with a thick horizontal stroke. She flipped it around.

"Oh, heaven help me," she breathed. Right there, in the center top of the page, sat a pink flamingo.

Neville's loafers scuffed on the pavement as he approached. "You all right, Henny?"

She shoved the paper into her purse and made a show of having difficulty standing. "Oh, my knees. Sorry. Once I get down, it's a lot harder to get back up these days."

"I know exactly what you mean." Neville laughed.

Inside, Henny tried to play it cool. She stared at the menu, not really seeing the words, her appetite snuffed out, thinking only of the paper in her purse—and what it meant.

Neville at the Pink Flamingo. Why? Did he take one of his dates there? Maybe Ruby? Or worse, did he use one of the poor girls employed at the White Lotus, or the Gilded Lily? Or even worse still, aid his buddy, Marshall McConner, in the trafficking?

Something else hit her. The notes. The one around the brick thrown through her window. The one on her car. Her heart rate increased to a near flutter. She took in a deep breath, attempting to clamp down on the fear, and keep a good poker face in place.

She fanned herself with her menu as the scent of hickory smoke and country ham assaulted her senses and sucked the air out of the already over-warm room.

"You all right?"

"Oh, yes. It's just really toasty in here, don't you think?"

Neville nodded. "A room this crowded, it's no surprise. What're you having? I'm thinking about meatloaf and mashed potatoes."

Henny played at studying the menu. "Oh, I-I don't know." She leaned one elbow on the table. "It all looks so good." *Calm down, Henny.* She inhaled a deep, silent breath. *Wait.* There must be an explanation. She searched her mind for a viable reason for Neville to have that paper in his car.

Think, Henny, think. Of course! Marshall McConner. Maybe Neville gave him a ride somewhere, and Marshall stuck the paper in the glove box for safekeeping and forgot to retrieve it. That thought helped to calm her somewhat, but still didn't shake her vague, unsettled feeling. She shifted in her chair. But . . . what if . . . what if it *did* belong to Neville?

The server approached to collect their order, and she tried to shove the thought away. She must survive dinner—then she didn't have to see Neville ever again.

Henny sneaked her phone out, and Neville, distracted with the server, didn't see her snap a picture of him. She could go by the Pink Flamingo motel later, see if anyone recognized him, and if so, break things off with Neville right then and there. If not, then she didn't need to worry. *Right?*

Having a plan of action eased Henny's mind, and she settled into her country ham, fried apples, collard greens, and cheesy shrimp grits. With each item she ate, her mind grew numb and more distant, while something inside her grew more excited. The same sort of feeling when she hit a yard sale.

After dinner, they stopped in the gift shop to pay the bill, and Henny stared at Neville's watch to keep from looking at all the holiday identity-crisis sections dedicated to autumn, Halloween, Thanksgiving, and Christmas. Her fingers itched while she fought the urge to look at only the sun catchers in the window, or the quilts, or the plates.

Neville signed the credit card receipt with a flourish, and she noticed how he wrote the "M" in Miller, three vertical lines with a thick horizontal stroke across the top, just like the writing on the motel stationery in his car. Her dinner felt like a stone in her stomach, and her body seized into something like rigor mortis.

Ohnoohnoohnoohno! Henny's heart threw itself against her chest like a wild animal in a trap, but she knew she needed to play it cool, and buy some time.

Neville stepped away from the counter, tucking the receipt in his wallet. Too late to make a run for the door.

"Um, I need to go to the restroom. I'll be right back." Henny dashed away, weaving through the crowded store, and ducked into the bathroom. She scanned the space. No windows. No other doors she might escape through, and no place to hide. *Great.* She removed her phone from her purse and called Sheriff Basham. No answer. She left a frantic message.

She dialed 9-1-1. The female operator answered in a steady,

professional tone.

Henny spoke in a shaky voice. "Help me. I'm in the bathroom at the Old Kentucky Kitchen near the interstate on the outskirts of Plumridge. I'm with Neville Miller, who may be involved in a human trafficking ring, and possibly two murders. Please send help immediately."

"Are you in any immediate danger?" Henny heard the sound of typing in the background.

"I don't know for sure."

"Okay, I'm sending help right away. Is he holding you against your will?"

"Well, no. But I fear he may be dangerous."

"Can you get away from him to a safe place?"

"I don't think I can. I'll try to stall him here at the restaurant. But I don't know for how long. Please hurry." Henny's head grew light as the bathroom seemed to grow bright and distant. She glanced at the mirror and didn't recognize herself, as if plucked out of her body and dropped into another one. What Dr. Phil might call a "dissociative state."

"Don't do anything to put yourself in danger."

"I understand."

"Can you stay on the line with me?"

A quick knock on the door, and it cracked open. Neville spoke from the other side. "Henny? You okay in there?"

"Almost. I'll be right out." Keeping her phone on, she tucked it into her bra, the microphone side up, in hopes that if something happened, there might be at least a recording of it for Ida Mae. Henny turned on the water and pretended to wash her hands. She ran a paper towel under the cold water and pressed it against her hot face to try to still her nerves.

Neville waited by the bathroom door when she exited. "Ready?" He smiled at her.

Henny smiled back. "I saw the cutest dishes in the window when we came in."

"Let's look another time. My belly's full, and I'm pretty tired now. You know how it is."

Dang it. "I understand. Do you care if I at least pick up a bag of those soft peppermint sticks? They're my favorite candy, and they might help your stomach too, if you have indigestion."

"Sure." His jaw knotted.

Henny moved in the opposite direction from the candy to take the longest way around. She stopped at a table of Christmas bird-houses, legitimately interested in them, and Neville sidled up to her. He put the candy in front of her.

"Here's the candy. You ready?"

"You found them. Aren't you a dear?" Henny pretended to search the room. "Where did you get those? I want to get a bag for my sister. She really likes them too."

Neville pointed to the corner across from the cash register. "They're over there."

Henny pretended she still didn't see them. "Where? I don't see them."

With a huff, he stepped through the crowd, and the various displays. He stood by the candy and waved. Henny made her way slowly toward the shelves.

He met her halfway with a bag. "Here you go." His tone seemed strained.

Henny stepped up to the cashier to pay. She fumbled with her wallet and money to buy some time, glancing out the large window for the deputies. She tried to meet the cashier's eyes to send a silent signal for help. Unfortunately, the young woman never looked up. Panic rose in Henny, as the cashier released a lifeless "Thank you," and turned away to address another customer. *Oh, heavens!*

"You ready?" Neville said. "Let's go."

Henny glanced out the window again. She learned on her detective shows to never let a dangerous man get her alone, or take her away from a public place, but she didn't want to show her hand. What should she do?

"Henny?" Neville's impatience ratcheted up a notch.

She knew she couldn't delay any longer, so she decided to follow him. She hoped the operator could hear her through the phone tucked in her bra.

She almost shouted, "Okay, I'll go with you to your car."

"Oookay. C'mon." Neville held the restaurant door open for her.

They stepped into the night air. The security lights reflected off the vehicles in the parking lot, lighting them up like multi-colored Christmas bulbs. As they approached his car, Henny bent down to look at the back, and adjusted her glasses to see better.

"What kind of car is this?" She read slowly, and loudly, in hopes the operator could hear. "Nissan. Altima."

Neville stood by the driver's door, the confusion etching his forehead in deep wrinkles.

She shouted, "I sure do like this gold color too. What year is this?"

"Why are you shouting?"

"Am I?"

"Yes."

"Oh, I didn't realize. My ears are all plugged up. Allergies. So what year is this car?"

"Does it matter? Get in." Neville opened the door and reached inside.

Henny searched the horizon for flashing lights and listened for distant sirens. She heard only traffic passing on the highway.

Neville approached her, and before she could register another thought, he clapped his arm around her shoulders, pulled her close, and jammed a pistol into her ribs.

He spoke close to her ear. "Let me be clear. You give me any problems, try to run, scream, or fight me, and I'll kill your sister while you watch. Slow and painful. Then I'll do the same to you. Got it?"

Henny shuddered, as fear trickled like ice water over her body. "I understand."

"Good girl." He walked her to the passenger side and closed her inside the car.

Tears slid down her face, and she swiped them away. She didn't want to think about how this might end. Henny tried to search for a bright spot, even one. Walter. Maybe they could truly be reunited soon. Maybe even see Lydia again. And Jenna. Forever young and beautiful. Henny didn't know the ghost world rules, but she could hope.

Henny's mind briefly visited the notion of Ida Mae without her, but she shoved that thought away. Too sad.

Neville got in the car and started it. He rested the gun in his lap. When he caught Henny looking at it, he said, "Careful. I hope you're not thinking of doing something incredibly stupid." He put the car into gear.

"I can't believe you're doing this to me, Neville Miller. You're just as evil as Marshall McConner, aren't you?'

He remained silent and pulled out of the spot.

"You stood there on my porch this evening and pretended you found trafficking evil and detestable. And the whole time you ran it."

Neville drove toward the parking lot exit, one hand on the steering wheel, one on the gun. "The more you talk, the worse it'll be for you. You best be making your peace with our Lord."

Henny heard faint sirens in the distance. "Why are we going North on I-75? That's opposite to my home."

He snapped. "Stop asking so many questions." Neville turned up the music. Tammy Wynette's "Stand By Your Man" blared.

Oh, for Pete's sake.

The sirens grew fainter. Maybe not for her at all. Maybe for a house fire, or a car wreck.

"Mile 18," she said.

"Wait . . . " He grabbed for her. "Are you wearing a wire?" He started feeling around on her body.

"Hey . . . " Henny, in a knee-jerk reaction, slapped at his hands like a high schooler on a first date. "You get your dirty paws off me."

The sirens faded. In their front seat tussle, Neville sped up, and swerved on the road. The gun slipped off his lap onto the floorboard. He cursed and leaned over to feel for it.

Henny couldn't allow Neville to get any further from town.

"Not tonight!" she shrieked. She grabbed the steering wheel and jerked it toward herself as Neville stepped on the gas in a panic. The car zipped off the asphalt onto the grass and down the embankment, bouncing and jerking their bodies. They ripped through a barbed wire fence, stopping in a recently harvested cornfield full of standing water from recent rains. Mud splashed up on the windshield, and the bleached and broken cornstalks stood like skeletons in the headlights.

Neville cursed her while still searching for his gun, and Henny saw her chance. She clawed for her door handle, popped it open, and spilled out onto the cold, wet mud. She pushed herself to her feet, and took off toward the embankment, the sludge sucking at her shoes. Finally, she heard sirens in the distance.

Neville got out of the car, shouting for her to stop, and slipping in the mud.

Henny glanced over her shoulder as he closed in on her. It felt like moving through wet concrete. Her lungs burned with the quick intake of oxygen. She came out of her shoes and left them behind. The mud could have them.

Neville reached out and grabbed her, pulling her back. She screamed and lost her footing. Henny fell to the ground, the air knocked completely out of her lungs.

"Shut up. Shut up," Neville growled, grabbing her around the neck as he reached back to hit her.

"Freeze!"

Another person shouted, "Put your hands up, jerk!"

Neville threw his hands in the air as Henny scrambled backward, away from him, the wet grass soaking into her dress, and the cold blades of grass poking her palms. Two men dressed in T-shirts, jeans, and work boots held hunting rifles pointed at Neville.

The shorter one with the scraggly beard said, "You're going to sit right there, buddy, until the sheriff gets here."

Neville tried to stand. "Buddy, you don't understand."

A tall, lanky guy in the camouflage ball cap said, "I understand I saw you beating up on some old lady . . . "

Henny didn't even mind that he called her old.

He continued, "You move one more muscle, and it'll be your last.

You just hang tight, lady."

The sirens closed in, and flashing lights popped over the hill. Henny clutched the grass. The cars screeched to a halt around the hunters who quickly put down their rifles, and the officers jumped out with their weapons drawn. Within moments, they descended around Neville and put him in cuffs as Henny watched the lights swirl around, coloring the night. She lay back in the grass, breathing in relief to still be alive.

"Oh, thank heavens," she sighed.

One of the good Samaritans approached. "Hey, lady. You okay?"

The burly man with a beard, dressed in bib overalls and a green John Deere cap, smelled like cherry tobacco. This couldn't be a coincidence. Walter somehow sent these brave young men to save her. She knew it.

He knelt to help her to her feet.

"Oh, thank you, son."

He looked her over. "You okay?"

"Yes. Yes, thank you. I am now. Thank you so much." Henny hugged him. She struggled to clamp down on the swirl of fear, relief, and gratitude. She teetered on the precipice of a complete emotional meltdown.

The young man helped her find her purse. In the grass, she noticed a small plastic flashlight. Probably from Neville's glove compartment. She could add it to her treasures as a memento of the night she almost died. Henny flicked the light on and off, on and off. Good, it still worked. An officer interrupted to ask Henny and the young men what happened. They all started talking at once. The officer held up a hand.

"One moment. Ma'am, after I talk to these gentlemen, I'll speak with you. In the meantime, let's get that arm looked at."

Henny looked down at the bleeding cut along her lower arm. Now that she noticed it, the pain and burning rose to the top. The deputy called over another officer, who escorted Henny to the ambulance to be treated by a paramedic.

She stumbled up the dewy embankment, the gravel on the

shoulder of the road rolling and crunching under her feet. Henny and the officer passed by Neville, now cuffed and leaning against a vehicle.

A slow, roiling rage rose up through her core. Henny jerked the zipper closed on her purse and clutched the straps in her hands. She marched toward Neville.

"Neville Miller!" she seethed. "You rotten, stinking, low-down..." She couldn't think of any more words. Instead, the rage launched her arm to swing her purse right across his cheek.

Neville grunted as his face snapped to the side.

The officer interviewing him hesitated, but didn't seem too eager to jump in.

"You pretended to be Walter's friend, then you tried to kill me," she shrieked, pulling the purse back again, this time walloping him in the chest. "And I know you killed my beloved Jenna, and Starla too."

"Ouch! I didn't have anything to do with that. Marshall did all that."

Henny shouted over him. "You took those poor people from their friends and families. You ought to rot in hell, mister. Did you ever even like me? Or did you just get close to me for information? Never mind, don't answer that. I don't think I want to know."

She lifted her purse to whack him again, but the officer stepped between them. "That's enough, Mrs. Wiley. Let's go get that cut treated now, and then we'll call someone to come get you."

Henny followed the deputy but shouted over her shoulder at Neville. "I hope you go to jail forever and rot there, you lying, scum-sucking, warthog."

He shouted back, "You shouldn't poke your nose where it doesn't belong, church lady!"

"That's enough," the deputy drawled, stepping in to block Henny's view.

"I meant every word," Henny muttered, jerking her purse into place on her shoulder.

Henny's arm required only minor first aid, so she gave her

statement, and turned over the Pink Flamingo stationery she found in Neville's car to a detective on the scene. "Check out that Miami address on the back," she said. "It could be a trafficking location."

Remembering her phone, she stuck her hand down her shirt, removed it from her bra, and called Ida Mae. "Can you come get me? And I'm going to need a change of clothes. And shoes."

24

Taking a break from raking, Henny sat in a lawn chair under an oak tree full of orangey-red leaves, enjoying a cup of hot cider. The sun shone bright, but the air felt cool. She needed the calming effect, and distraction of the work, despite the aching in her body from last night's events.

Ida Mae pulled up, and Khan barked. All seemed right in Henny's world. "There's apple cider in the house, if you want some." Henny said.

"I think I will."

Henny pulled a lawn chair from the shed and set it up near hers.

Ida Mae, back with her cider, sat down with a soft grunt.

They sipped their drinks. Ida Mae broke the silence first. "How're you feeling?"

"Okay, I guess. I spoke with Mr. Lawson, and invited him to church with us on Sunday, so that made me feel better, but I didn't sleep too well. Lots of nightmares from last night."

"Sounds pretty traumatic from what you told me."

Walter lay on the pile of leaves, his arms behind his head. "I told you not to mess around with Neville."

Henny glared at him, then she softened, remembering that time he told her not to lend money to her no-good brother, Cash, and she never saw a dime in return. Walter never let her live that down.

She thought of that verse in Proverbs. Something about a fool trusts his own heart, but a person who walks in wisdom . . .

Wait. How is trusting the heart and wisdom different? The rest of the verse perched on the tip of her tongue.

"Are you all right, Henny?"

"I'm really sore. I'm too old to be running around and getting tackled to the ground."

"I can't believe Neville Miller is a human trafficker. Boy, did he fool us."

"Not me," Walter said.

Henny snapped her head around and gave him "The Look."

He stuck out his tongue and laughed.

Henny poked him with the rake.

Ida Mae craned her neck. "What're you doing over there?"

"Thought I saw a chipmunk. Can you imagine Neville as the ring-leader? I can't."

Ida Mae twisted in her chair, almost spilling her cider. "You're kidding?"

"I wish. He coordinated the capture, and transfer, of laborers and . . . " She didn't want to say it. "You know. The girls. His ring ran from Ohio and Illinois, to Kentucky, and Florida."

"My Lord." Ida Mae sipped her drink.

"And you know that paper from the motel?"

"Yes."

"I found the exact same stationery in Neville's car. And when the deputies arrested him, I turned it over to them. Sheriff Basham called me this morning and said they looked into that Miami address after I asked them to, and guess what?"

"What?"

"They found a bunch of trafficked people from the Gilded Lily and the White Lotus there, including Angel, the girl we saw behind the spa that day. She's safe and reunited with her parents. She even asked the sheriff for my number, so she can call me. Isn't that terrific?"

"Henny, that's great, but remember she's not your daughter, okay?"

"I know, I know. Don't worry. But isn't it a miracle I gave Jenna an angel and she gave her life so an Angel could be saved?"

"Yes, Henny, that's really something, isn't it?" Ida Mae patted her sister's arm. After a few moments of silence, Ida Mae crossed her ankles and relaxed deeper into her chair. "I guess yard sale season is officially over."

"Yep." Henny sipped her now lukewarm cider. "There's always Christmas bazaars, and indoor flea markets though."

Ida Mae squinted up at the sun through the treetops. "You know, I'm thinking I might do some fall cleaning, and clear out all my junk." She made a nudging motion toward the house. "Hint, hint."

Henny ignored her. "You don't have any junk."

"Sure, I do. My garage, and attic, and that third bedroom."

"You don't have half the stuff I do."

"That's true, but I noticed yesterday, I'm starting to get really cluttered. So, I think I'm going to get rid of a bunch of it. Maybe have a big yard sale in the spring."

"You need to do that too, Henny!" Walter called out.

"Don't start with me," she hissed at him.

Ida Mae sat up and craned her head. "Who're you talking to?"

"I'm talking to you."

"While looking over there?" Ida Mae pointed.

"I thought I saw the chipmunk again."

After casting a suspicious look at her sister, Ida Mae relaxed once more. "Anyway, maybe you want to go through your stuff too, and in the spring, we can have a huge yard sale. Just think about it. That's all I'm asking. We can take the fall and winter to decide."

Walter laughed.

Henny stood and grabbed the rake, poking Walter with it.

"Quit that!" He vanished and reappeared on the porch.

Henny suppressed her smile. "I need to finish raking."

Ida Mae helped with the gathering, then left to go home. Henny stood behind the shed, adding fresh leaves to a barrel of fire. She stared at the flames. She knew she should apologize to Walter. Her mind, clouded by loneliness, and her ego, flattered by thinking a man might once again be interested in her, failed her. She felt invisible.

Like a ghost.

Henny threw in the last heaping handful of leaves. Crows settled in the nearly naked trees and squawked loudly, heralding the Halloween season. The smoke filled the air, and the fire warmed her face. She should probably try to find the Halloween decorations and decorate the house for Walter. Henny couldn't compete with the houses down the street, but why not make for a welcoming atmosphere for the trick-or-treaters visiting soon.

She needed a change. A new and improved Henny who wore different clothes, and a different hairstyle, and attitude—a whole new life designed to build up her confidence. After all, Dr. Phil said a confident woman is an attractive woman. She put a lid over the barrel to snuff the fire and marched toward the house. Her house. Walter's house. *Their* house.

Yes, a whole new Henny.

Henny threw open the back door, and stood in the kitchen, surveying the empty cans and containers on the table, countertops, and floor. Bags and boxes filled with goodies stood against the walls, some as tall as Henny, five feet, five inches.

She picked up a shopping bag and placed a few empty cans inside. The first can sent a thrill through her that felt both like fear and excitement—like that time she rode the Ferris wheel at the state fair.

Henny grabbed a few magazines from the chair. Maybe she could toss a few of those. Take them to the recycling center in the morning. She grew a little dizzy, as though she stood up too quickly. After four passes, and two hours, she managed to stuff just four magazines into the bag. She blew out a shaking breath.

"Just one more. I can do one more." Though she felt nauseous, she reached for the lid of a bakery box, and opened it.

Henny's heart swelled as she removed one of the items inside. She held the porcelain angel she'd bought for Jenna, running her thumbs over the carved feathers.

She smiled to herself at the *I'm thinking of you* of sorts from the world beyond. Energized now, she tucked the angel carefully back in the box alongside the angel earrings and carried the bag of old magazines to her truck where she dropped the bundle into the bed. Henny stood on her tiptoes and touched the bag. The crows cried out and cut through the sky. Khan barked. A scent of cherry tobacco lingered in the air. She looked at the bag and touched it again.

Henny blew out a breath and stepped away from the truck.

ACKNOWLEDGMENTS

All glory to God always. Ephesians 3:20

I would like to thank my editors, Kent Holloway and Britin Haller, Chrissy Smith, and the rest of the Charade Media team for taking a chance on Henny and finding the diamond in the rough. I really appreciate the work, care, and dedication you all have devoted to this strange little book. More than anything, I'm thankful to be a partner!

I'm especially thankful to family and friends—you all know who you are. I'm ever grateful for your support, encouragement, and love. I love you all and when I think of you I understand how deeply and beautifully blessed I am!

A special shout out to...

Brack, my moon and stars. My knight in shining armor.

None of this is possible without you. My life is infinitely better with you in it.

Carmen Erickson, you're the best critique partner and a wonderful friend. You hold my hand in the storms. You understand the good, the bad, and the ugly. And I appreciate you.

Also, Hallie Lee. I'm so thankful for you and your friendship. Our lunches are so special and I look forward to them with delight. I appreciate you and look forward to sharing lots of book fairs together!

To my readers, you are the greatest blessing because you make writing possible and worth it! It's always my greatest hope and my greatest joy when my work can bring a few hours of happiness and entertainment to you. Thank you a thousand times for your support!

ABOUT THE AUTHOR

Born and raised in the beautiful Bluegrass state of Kentucky, **Michelle Bennington** developed a passion for books early on that has progressed into a mild hoarding situation and an ever-growing to-read pile. She delights in spinning mysteries and histories. Find out more on her website: www.michellebennington.com and follow her on Facebook, Instagram, Twitter, and Goodreads.